Twenty Questions

ALSO BY ALISON CLEMENT

Pretty Is As Pretty Does

Twenty Questions

A NOVEL

Alison Clement

ATRIA BOOKS

NEW YORK · LONDON · TORONTO · SYDNEY

ATRIA BOOKS

1230 Avenue of the Americas
New York, NY 10020

ISBN-13: 978-0-7432-7266-7
ISBN-10:   0-7432-7266-8

First Atria Books hardcover edition July 2006

3   5   7   9   10   8   6   4   2

ATRIA B O O K S is a trademark of Simon & Schuster, Inc.

Manufactured in the United States of America

For information regarding special discounts for bulk purchases,
please contact Simon & Schuster Special Sales at 1-800-456-6798 or
business@simonandschuster.com

For my mother, Mari Dunavan Clement

Twenty Questions is a common grade school guessing game in which one player selects an object and the other players may each ask up to twenty questions in order to identify it. The principles of Twenty Questions can be used in any problem-solving situation where the problem is associated with a single element of a complex system.

Twenty Questions

Chapter 1

*I*t started the day she opened the paper and saw Ralphie Pruett's father. She knew then that she was alive only because she had said no to him, and so he went and got some other woman and killed her instead.

The paper was in the staff room, left over from the teachers at lunch. June spread it out flat on the table and looked at it. She started to reach for a cigarette, but she was in school and so she stopped herself. She had finished her shift and was ready to go home. She took her apron off while she read the article.

His name was Ronald Pruett. He had killed the girl last Wednesday; on Saturday the body had been found, and he had been arrested. The article didn't say where the girl's body was when they found it. Sometimes, June thought, it's a shallow grave and sometimes it's a place like the garage. She thought of her own garage with its concrete floor. You couldn't very well bury someone in a garage like that. And she got sidetracked and stuck on the idea of the garage, the dark garage full of old dirty things, plastic gallon containers of automotive fluid, old lamps and broken appliances, and an old car or two. She was stuck there. She didn't think of the girl, Vernay Hanks, yet. Vernay was just a waitress at Darrel's Hamburgers, although they weren't really called waitresses, just a girl who needed a ride.

She folded up her apron and put it away. She grabbed her pocketbook and walked out the back door. She walked through the empty playground, through the parking lot and to her car; the car that broke down over on Jackson Street last Wednesday. Jackson Street was named after Andrew Jackson who had his belts made from the skin of Indians: an obsessive thought she never failed to have whenever she heard his name, a monster. The old fuel pump went out right there on that street with the unfortunate name, and then Ralphie's father stopped.

He had a blue pickup with mag wheels and a beige fender where it had been replaced and they had used the wrong color. He stopped and offered her a ride. He was just as nice as could be. She couldn't place him right away, and then she did, from when he waited in the hallway for Ralphie after school sometimes. She usually said yes when people insisted, but that day she didn't.

He had gotten out of his truck and looked under her hood. They were on a street with big, old, well-built houses: houses that people used to know how to make before the dark ages when everyone forgot what they knew, or just didn't care about it anymore. June had never been inside one of those houses. No one she knew lived here.

None of the students lived here. None of the teachers. The Pruetts, of course, didn't live here.

Ralphie's father had left his truck running, like he was in too big a hurry to turn it off, and from the sound of it, that truck needed a muffler.

When someone stops to help with your car, it's hard not to feel obligated to watch what they are doing, June thought. You feel you should watch even if you don't know a thing about it or care. She had tried to tear her eyes away from the houses and aim them instead beneath her hood, where the father of one of the students, she hadn't remembered which one yet, twisted and pulled and wiggled his hands around.

One of the houses had its blinds up and the lights on. She could see the dining room table from where she stood. She could see a chandelier, a wooden high chair, a tall vase of flowers, a silver candlestick holder, a painting on the wall. June wanted to walk up the steps and open the front door to that house. She wanted to go inside and sit at the table. She wanted to light the candle and sit in one of the wooden chairs, waiting for dinner. She wanted to hold the baby on her lap.

She thought about when she was young and might have married someone who could have given her a house like this one. She might have married Sean Callahan who had his own airplane, but she didn't.

June didn't like conflict. If pressed she'd usually say yes, but she hadn't said yes to Sean, and she didn't say yes to Mr. Pruett either, even though he had been so nice and then so insistent. She didn't want a ride. Truly. She wanted to walk along Jackson Street in the late afternoon, by herself. She would walk into downtown and catch a bus.

June wasn't a dreamy woman, and she wasn't restless, and June loved her husband, Bill. *Bill, I love you so I always will.* It was an old Laura Nyro song. June could never say the name of her husband without thinking of it, another obsessive thought but this time harmless. Sometimes she'd sing it to him, and she meant it. Bill.

If June ever imagined having a different kind of life, it was always with Bill. Remembering it now, it seemed that she had had a strange feeling that day. She had felt oddly alive in those moments, standing by the car, strangely excited, almost as if something in her knew how close she was to the end. It stood right there. A fork in the road had been reached, and she had been only one misstep away from a grave in someone's garage.

People came into the kitchen, a teacher, an assistant. The custodian came in, and usually she would talk to him, but that day she didn't. Ralphie's father was a secret, and he would be a secret until the moment she told Bill, and then finally she would know what it meant. She would know by what she felt when she said it, by how it sounded to her, by what he said back, and by what she said back again. Until then it was a mystery.

June drove home from work telling herself, I was lucky. It could have been me, but it wasn't. She didn't let herself think of the other woman. She had skimmed that part of the article. It had been that woman instead of her, and she was glad, there was no getting around it. She was glad to be alive driving her car down the road with the sky above her, with her arms and legs and her whole body, breathing and sitting and looking, feeling and thinking. The nuns used to say that the body is a temple, and that seemed right to June. Her body was a temple, and it was alive; but the other woman, her body was lying on a slab somewhere. It was in a drawer in a cold room; it had a tag tied around the toe, or maybe that was only in the movies. It could have been me, June thought, and she began to shake.

Bill had left a roach in June's ashtray, which in plain English meant the leftover end of a marijuana cigarette, and she lit it. She smoked it even though she had just come from work, which was at a school, and was still in her work frame of mind, which was wholesome, more or less. When you work in a grade school, you become wholesome, and you say *oh my goodness* when you're excited, instead of *Jesus Christ,* and you stop saying *shit* and *goddamn it* altogether, June thought.

Ralphie's father had kept asking, and she had kept saying no. She had been pretty far from home, and it was almost dusk. Maybe she would have relented finally, but then a woman came out of one of the houses. She walked down the stairs toward her car. She said hello to them, and she looked at them both. She had spent enough time there to identify Mr. Pruett in a police lineup, maybe, although identifying people for the police is harder than you might think, June had heard. The mind doesn't like a vacuum. If there's a blank, the mind will fill it in. If you don't remember a nose, the mind will find one for you and stick it there and that nose, which is something the mind made up itself and should recognize as a lie, will be as true to the mind as the honest to God truth. Why take a chance, Ronald Pruett must have thought, when there are so many other women everywhere? Maybe I'll go by Darrel's Hamburgers instead.

Ralphie Pruett was pale and skinny. He was a mean boy. You knew what kind of man he'd grow up to be, but you couldn't hold that against him. So far he was just little, six years old. He had tiny perfect ears and little fingers that clutched his plastic food tray and then reached to put corn dogs on it, and other things that would kill you.

Somewhere in the food that Ralphie Pruett ate there were remnants of real food. There was a pig, and corn that grew in a field. And somewhere in Ralphie was the perfect being that we all are. In Ralphie, with his dirty fingernails, his sallow skin, waxy ears, whiny voice, and wary eyes, his shoving and his thickness—somewhere there was the boy he could have been if someone loved him and gave him something decent to eat every now and then. It's surprising, June had thought more than once, how little is actually required.

Before you work at a school, you think you know what children are. You think children have small worries, sleep at night in warm beds with stuffed animals, eat meals at a table with their families, have fathers and mothers who love them. Before you work at a school, you think you know what parents are. You imagine parents like your own parents: not perfect, but people who fed you and cared if you did your homework, people who made sure the bills were paid and there was a refrigerator in the house, with food.

Usually on her way home from work, June listened to the news, but today she didn't think she could bear it: every day some new disaster, as if she was suddenly in a Doris Lessing novel, one of her series about the end of civilization. Just when it seemed that nothing else could go wrong, it did, and now there was the war. The kids talked about it all the time. "We are winning," they told her. They had heard this at home, she knew—but how could anyone call what was happening in Iraq winning? Unless it was a killing contest. If it was a killing contest, they were winning hands down. She thought, The only thing that stands between me and the world is Bill. She would tell him that when he got home.

June put on the music station, and Steve Earle was singing a song he had written about capital punishment.

Send my Bible home to mama
Call her every now and then

June had mixed feelings about capital punishment. When a man in Portland killed a six-year-old boy, she was for it, but when she listened to Steve Earle sing his song, she was against it.

People said that anybody could be redeemed, but June didn't believe that. Maybe, she thought, a man doesn't deserve to be redeemed. Maybe sometimes he just goes too far. Maybe sometimes a man gets to be like a mad dog; the best you can do is take him out back and shoot him, that's all.

June thought of Mr. Pruett, and she wondered if he could be redeemed. She wondered what he had thought after he killed the woman. What had he done next? Did he just go in and wash his hands and eat dinner? She thought of the politicians who chose war, knowing what it meant: murder and mayhem, blood, guts, horror, and death. They chose war and then talked about it on TV in their clean white shirts, smiling, and then the next minute sat down to eat dinner. No one blamed them for being cold-blooded.

She tried to remember exactly what Ralphie's father had looked like, where he had stood, how he had moved, what he had said, everything about him, no matter how small. She tried to find some clue, but she couldn't. You'd think if you stood right next to someone who was prepared to strangle you, you'd notice something out of place. People reveal small things about themselves in countless ways, June thought, but somehow she had stood next to Ralphie's father, with his unspeakable plans, and she had only thought of her car. She had tried to be polite and helpful. She had thought of the street where they stood and the houses nearby. She had felt oddly alive, but what kind of clue was that?

June parked her car and ran up the front steps and into her house. She was barely in the door when she started telling Bill the story. The paper said he had strangled her. June hadn't even taken her coat off. She stood in the kitchen doorway, talking quickly, barely seeing him. She watched his hands, as they covered a dish of pasta salad with foil. She had been talking, but now she stopped. She had only gotten to the part where the woman in a red coat had come out of her house and seen them both looking into the engine of her car.

She wondered about the red coat. Was it something real from that day, or something her imagination had inserted? She wanted to tell it all, everything she could remember, plus everything she remembered but might have only imagined. She stood in the doorway and looked at the yellow daffodils on the table and relayed the story to Bill, but Bill exclaimed, "Wait a minute, baby! Just hold on a minute!"

He said she needed to calm down. Calm down, relax. She was all wound up. He put the bowl of pasta in the refrigerator and turned to her. Was she sure it was the same man? Was she positive? It was the same day? "Oh, my God." He pulled her to him, saying, "There, there, shhh, it will be all right. Never take a ride from someone you don't know, June." He was just glad she was safe. He put his finger to her lips and said, "What do you think, it's your fault the other girl was killed?" He said, "Things happen, and we don't know why." He said, "Come here, baby. Come here," and he put his arms around her, and she leaned into his chest. If anybody ever touched her, he'd kill them.

She wanted to tell the whole story from the beginning to the middle to the end. She sat down at the kitchen table and started again, with the woman in the coat. He sat across from her, listening. He was a good listener. He let her talk. She knew he had to go to work soon, but he didn't look at his watch. When she was finished, he told her she ought to call her friend Louise. "Don't sit around here, being morbid. Go have some fun." He always thought she should go have fun, whatever that meant.

"I don't want to have fun!"

She followed him into the bedroom, and he got ready for work. June sat on the bed, watching him dress. He wore good black pants and a white shirt to work even though he was the cook, the chef, back in the kitchen where no one saw him.

Bill was a handsome man. He was tall, 6' 2", and muscular. He had thick black hair and dark eyes, long eyelashes, and broad, capable hands, cooking hands, he called them. He was the kind of man women liked to talk to, a man who knew how to listen. He came from Chicago. His mother was Italian, and his father was a bricklayer. Bill was dark like his mother, and strong like his father. He was raised Catholic like June, but he had never believed it, not for one minute.

June's own father was dead, and her mother was still back in Greenville, South Carolina. June had one brother, but he was in Texas. She had always wanted a big family, like the other kids at school. She went to Catholic school, Holy Rosary—Holy Roller, they had called it, for a joke. The other kids had big families, a child in every grade it seemed like, but for June there was just her and her brother.

Bill and June had been married ten years, but she liked to watch him, and she liked to hear what he had to say. If she was in a crowded room and someone was talking to her, it didn't matter who that person was, if she heard Bill's voice, she strained to hear what he was saying.

He buttoned his shirt, watching her. Then suddenly he thought about the dead girl and said, "Fucking nuts out there. I'd like to get my hands on them."

June liked to sit outside on the back steps but it was just April, and the days were still too cold so, after Bill left for work, she sat at the kitchen table. He had made dinner for her, and it was in the refrigerator. It was conventional wisdom that plumbers' wives could never get their plumbing fixed and the families of construction workers lived in half-built homes. Whatever your husband did at work, you couldn't expect him to do it around the house. But Bill loved to cook for her. He loved to feed her, and he loved to watch her eat. In a few more years they would both be fat.

She drank a glass of red wine and looked out the window. It had been a dry spring, but the days had been cloudy and often a thick, wet fog had settled over the town. Oregon needed rain, everyone said, but June hated the rain. It had been sunny the day Ralphie's father had stopped—a good day for walking. If it had been raining, if there had been clouds or fog, would she have taken the ride?

June looked out the window at the house next door. The neighbors had been fighting, but that night they were quiet.

Her friend Louise called, but June didn't say anything about Ralphie's father. She locked the door and sat on the couch, but she didn't turn on the TV or read. She sat quietly, and she did not think morbid thoughts about being buried in a garage with old tires. She didn't think of the dead woman or Ralphie's father, although something in her kept trying to bring them to mind.

Some people said everything happened for the best, but June didn't believe that, not for a minute. People said everything happens the way it should, but that wasn't true either. People said all kinds of things, but it was only to hide from facts, and June didn't want to hide from facts. She told herself that the opportunity for pain in the past and in the future was limitless, but that we need to look at what is here, right now, that's all.

June looked around the room. She was sitting on an old purple velvet couch. The floors were wood. The walls were pale yellow, a warm color, and the ceiling was white. The ceiling was high. It was an old duplex, and the couple next door had just moved in and they fought. The TV was across from her. She had picked daffodils the day before and set a bouquet in a mason jar on the coffee table. Yellow was her favorite color but it hadn't always been. She wasn't going to think of anything in the past, even if it was just what her favorite color had been. She looked at the flowers. She breathed in and out.

Chapter 2

*I*t was spring, and the kids had spring fever. As soon as the doors opened they'd burst outside screaming and jumping, and some of them would hit each other and cry because they were just children, and sometimes they didn't know what to do with their strong feelings. June walked across the parking lot. She walked past the empty playground. There was some garbage blowing around, but she didn't stop to pick it up. She unlocked the door to the kitchen and went in.

In the rest of the school, the teachers and assistants, the specialists and the secretary, were all friendly with each other; but down in the kitchen, it was just June and the kids. The school sent the bad kids to June, so they could be socialized. They might end up working in a kitchen anyhow, the lucky ones, but nobody said that.

The kids ate their meals in the gym, which was directly outside the kitchen. Nearly every child in the school was from a family poor enough to make them eligible for the government's free or reduced lunch program. The school provided breakfast, as well.

On the other side of town the parents were engineers. They worked at Hewlett-Packard or the university, and they could buy their own food, but here at George Washington Elementary School the children got free Cocoa Puffs or sticky buns for breakfast.

The children ate at long folding tables which the custodian, Frank Nguyen, set up for them. Their voices echoed in the big room. After they finished eating, they cleaned up their area. They wiped down the table, picked up everything they had dropped or spilled on the floor, and ran to wait by the double doors that led to the rest of the building. Every morning they waited by those doors, pushing forward, sometimes prematurely breaking free to run for a moment down the hallway, like teenagers at a rock concert.

It was lunchtime and June stood at the counter waiting for the first class. Mikey Black was on one side of her and Missy, a girl with an eye patch, was on the other. The kids wore plastic aprons and plastic gloves, to prevent germs. They were serving wiener wraps, everybody's favorite. Two days earlier Mikey's mother had taken off, leaving him with Grandma, but today he looked the same as ever. He said, "Didja hear about Cindy's mom?"

Missy leaned around June to say, "I was just over to her house, and I seen her mom that day."

"Didja hear what happened to her?" asked Mikey.

"Cindy Hanks, you mean?" asked June, but she already knew the answer. The paper had given the victim's name,

Vernay Hanks. She had read the name, but she hadn't thought of Cindy. She had thought Vernay. Now what kind of name is that? Is it French or did they make it up? She had turned down the ride, and he had gone on to the next woman—Cindy's mother, Vernay Hanks.

Missy used her one eye to glare at Mikey. "Of course I heard. I heard before you."

Mikey didn't argue with her. He turned to June instead. "Ralphie's father got her, and now he's in jail."

"She's my cousin," said Missy, but this was a lie, and they ignored it.

"Did you hear what he did to her?" asked Mikey.

"I know," said June quickly. She thought of Cindy Hanks, in trouble last week for pushing in line, a lively, black-haired, curly-headed girl, a fifth grader. A girl on free lunch.

Missy said, "They found her in the woods, and she was—"

"Missy!" Maybe she was supposed to let the kids process this, but she didn't want to.

"Now she's with Jesus," said Missy.

"One thing we don't have to worry about is zombies, Mrs. Duvall. Some people think dead people turn into zombies and walk among us, but it's not true. It's made up," said Mikey.

"It's fiction," said Missy.

And Mikey had an additional optimistic thought. "It's lucky we'll never be hit by a comet," he said.

Mikey was a handsome, well-made boy with pale blue

eyes, smooth, pink cheeks, and a blond crew cut. His hands were always dirty and his fingernails bitten down to the quick. He was a sensitive boy who cried easily and dressed in camouflage. His teacher said he didn't have a father, but this was just a way of talking. He was a fourth grader, nine years old. He wanted to be a soldier, he told June.

You weren't supposed to give your political opinions to the children, but when it came to war June couldn't stop herself. "Wars are sad," she told him. "So many people get hurt and killed in wars."

It wasn't the children of the rich who went to war, she knew, it was children like the ones in her school. It was the poor who fought the wars, one raw deal leading to another. "I thought you were going to be an astronomer," she said. "You know all about the planets and comets."

But he wouldn't hear of it. "Baghdad is bad!" he told her.

The kids always came in in alphabetical order, holding their plastic trays while June and Mikey and Missy put things on them; bad things, poisonous things that would give them cancer one day, June thought, but she had been round and round with the school district and had gotten nowhere. They were ready, in position, but the kids were having a hard time coming in, and the teacher had stopped them outside the door. She could hear them stamping their feet like little horses. She could hear them talking, and she could hear them telling each other *Shut up!*

Missy said, "If we didn't have pupils, we wouldn't be able to see."

And they stood quietly, the three of them together, thinking of this lucky thing, pupils.

Finally Mikey turned to June. "Don't you wish we could stay like this forever?"

"What do you mean?"

"I mean, isn't this nice."

They were standing side by side in front of a counter holding aluminum trays of wiener wraps.

"It's fun to work with you," she said. She could feel Missy pressing in on the other side of her, and so June turned to include her. "If this was my restaurant, I'd hire you both."

At other schools they might have grief counseling, and the kids would draw pictures and hold teddy bears when a classmate's mother was found murdered, but at George Washington Elementary School, there was nothing extra to go around. Washington was the poor school, and it was a bad year for schools anyway. The district was threatening to close schools, and Washington was next on the chopping block. They all called it *chopping block*. At other schools, parents organized committees and met the school board. They had petitions and yard signs, "Keep our school open." They wrote letters to the paper. But at George Washington Elementary School, the parents were used to getting shoved around. They had enough to worry about already, and they didn't let out a peep. So when Ralphie's father was arrested, no one thought to call a counselor or have him draw pictures of how he was feeling. When Cindy's mother was found, no one had more than a moment of regret to give her.

Each class took turns lining up in alphabetical order. A–Z. It had been six days since Vernay Hanks had died instead of June. Now Exhibit A. The fifth grade class was first in line: Amos, Anderson, Brown and eventually Cindy Hanks who was not there.

"She's gone missing," said Brittanee Dupree.

"Yes, yes, her mother's dead, and she's missing," said another girl.

"It was Ralphie's father that done it," said a freckled boy named Fred. Freddy Freckles the kids called him, and now they all forgot about Cindy and her dead mother and Ralphie's bad father, because Victor had begun to push.

Gone missing, that can mean moved. She had gone to Grandma probably. The kids went to Grandma usually. They almost never went to their fathers. If it wasn't Grandma or an aunt, then they would have put Cindy in foster care. There must be some kind of short list in foster care, for emergencies like this one.

Once the school had two little sisters who were taken away from their parents, and that same day social workers asked everyone on the staff if they could take one or both of them. A parent has to do a lot for that to happen, June had learned. Children like that, the ones who are most harmed, they bite and scratch and wet their pants sometimes. When you hear a story like theirs, you think you'd take the poor child, but then it happens, and you don't.

Maybe right now the same thing was happening with Cindy. Maybe social workers were telling the staff that the normal requirements could be waived. Or maybe something else had happened, and Cindy really had gone missing.

As soon as lunch was finished, June walked out of the kitchen. She walked through the gym past the custodian, Mr. Nguyen, who was stacking the long folding tables where the children ate. She walked down the hall, wiping her hands on her white apron. She passed the graphs kids had made showing how they got to school: walk, bus, car, bike. She passed the maps the fifth graders had made. She passed the bilingual classroom with its bright banners, and she turned, finally, into the office.

She was surprised to see two police officers. She almost ran into one of them, a young man in a blue uniform, who stood by the door with a gun in his holster. When did cops start looking like kids? she wondered.

"I suppose you're working on the Hanks case?" she asked. But he didn't want to tell her what case they were working on. He might look like a child, but he didn't have to answer her.

A fourth-grade teacher and an assistant stood at the copy machine, while the other cop, who looked like Joe Friday from the old *Dragnet* series, talked to Mrs. Lipski, the school secretary. He had a small pad of paper, in which he wrote things as Mrs. Lipski spoke.

"Do you know where Cindy Hanks is?" June asked the women at the copy machine.

The teacher said, "I heard Cindy's staying with her uncle." And then she added, "I guess he works down at the salvage yard," which was off the point.

"Poor girl, she's had more than her share of trouble," said the assistant. And then she lowered her voice. "I guess, on top of everything else, there's been incest in that family."

But this kind of information was confidential, and the teacher said quickly, "She and her mother have been living with the uncle."

"That wasn't in the paper," said June.

But the teacher was firm about the uncle, and she and the assistant began to wonder out loud if the uncle would get custody of poor little Cindy, and if not, where would she go, and isn't it a shame, and don't we wish we could take them all home, but God knows we can't.

June walked to the secretary's desk. She should wait her turn, she knew, but she had things to do. She had to clean up the kitchen. She had to get back to her helpers, alone now, washing dishes. She could trust Mikey and Missy to do their jobs, but still you didn't want to leave them alone for more than a moment.

"Where's Cindy Hanks?" she asked. "The kids say she's gone missing."

Mrs. Lipski and Joe Friday turned to her.

"Do you need her for something?" Joe Friday asked, looking doubtfully at June in her ponytail and white apron.

June paused.

"Is she a lunchroom helper?" asked the fourth-grade teacher helpfully, and June looked at her blankly for just an instant before answering that yes, as a matter of fact, Cindy *was* a lunchroom helper.

Cindy was absent, Mrs. Lipski said, which meant missing, but with different connotations.

Joe Friday closed up his notebook and put his pen in his front pocket. "We'd like a quick word with you," he said to June.

For an irrational moment, she thought they knew about her and Ralphie's father, but that couldn't be right. June stepped into the hallway with them. Joe Friday asked if Cindy Hanks had said anything about her mother's death to June, but June said no, she hardly knew Cindy, and she hadn't seen her at all since the murder.

But then June added, "I did see Ralphie's father—Mr. Pruett—the day she was killed."

The men stepped in closer, and Joe Friday reached into his pocket for the notebook. She wondered if she was supposed to have reported her encounter with Mr. Pruett to the police earlier, and she was struck by the fact that the thought of it hadn't occurred to her. But then, she told herself, it wasn't like she had an alibi for Ronald Pruett. An alibi is when someone was somewhere else and couldn't have committed the crime. What she had was just part of the story of Ronald Pruett's day.

After she had finished describing what had happened, they asked for her name, her phone number and address. "I've already told you everything I know," she protested. But they needed these things, they said.

After work June drove to the Hankses' house. It was three blocks from school, on a street of trailers and small houses. The trailers were rusted, and the houses needed paint. There was stuff in all the yards, old toys and boxes, rusted tools and garbage cans. Even though it was April, the yard across the street had a life-size plastic Santa lying on its side. Next to the Santa, a barking dog pulled on a cord.

Cindy's house was old. It had a front porch with a broken handrail. It had two cars in the driveway; one was up on blocks. June could see a man underneath it; his legs were sticking out. She pulled her car to the curb and sat, but she didn't turn the engine off at first. It had stopped raining, but it was chilly, and she wore a coat and a scarf around her neck. A fat brown Chihuahua came out from under Cindy's porch and barked, and June got out of the car and walked toward the man. The front door to the house across the street opened up, and the neighbor stuck his head out. "Shut up!" he yelled at his dog. "Shut the fuck up!"

June wasn't sure what she was going to say. She hadn't planned it out, but she wasn't worried. The Chihuahua followed her up the driveway, but she wasn't worried about the dog either. She got to the car that was up on blocks and stopped. She hadn't taken her apron off, but she had a coat over it, and now she pulled that coat around her and waited while he pushed himself out from under the car and sat up, looking at her. June had thought that as soon as she saw him she'd know what she wanted to say, but so far she didn't. He was a handsome man, a man who could surely find a woman, if he wanted a woman, but some men, apparently, want children. What makes them think what they want is so important? she wondered, looking at him.

He had the solid jaw and black eyebrows of Cindy. He had high cheekbones and blue eyes. Except for the color of his eyes, he looked like a Mongolian, like a man from a *National Geographic* article about Mongolia where the people look like Indians and ride ponies with no hands, or was that the Apache? He looked like he could do anything, and she didn't trust competence like that. He sat looking at her. He wiped his face with the back of his hand and left a grease mark across his cheek and temple.

She looked across the street at the dirty old Santa lying on its side, and she wondered what kind of people would just leave it there, walking around it every day for all these months instead of dragging it off. She looked back down at the man, and she resented him for living in plain sight of such a ridiculous, ugly-looking thing.

"This your car?" she asked.

He shook his head like something was flying around it, bothering him. "What of it?"

"Is it broke?"

"Who are you?" he asked. He looked at her clothes now, to see if they gave a clue, but her apron was hidden beneath her coat, and there was nothing to see. He looked down at her practical shoes, but anybody could wear shoes like that. "Are you a social worker?"

June felt a pang of regret. If she had thought this out carefully beforehand, then she might have come up with a useful plan.

"No."

Most men were usually happy to let her interrupt them,

but Cindy's uncle was the impatient type. He lay back on the ground. He had a piece of cardboard under him, and he slid back under the car. Anybody would have been curious at least, but maybe he was too dull to be curious, June thought. She squatted down next to his feet and bent her head to the side, trying to see him, but she couldn't.

"I'm a friend of your sister's," she said.

He didn't come out from under the car. "She's dead, you know."

June waited. She could see his arm move where he was twisting something around. She moved her head back up, but she was still squatting. Any minute Cindy might come out of the house. June looked up at the house, but she didn't see anybody.

"We were good friends, Vernay and me," she told him, getting a little carried away. "But then lately we sort of lost touch." The little dog sniffed her leg, but June didn't kick it away. "You know how that is." It didn't feel like a lie and June wondered if lies were usually like this—once spoken, did they always begin to seem like the truth? She thought of the kids at school and their earnest, passionate lies. "It was such a shock," June added. "Vernay was a wonderful girl."

She hesitated. "I work at Cindy's school," she said, and she was surprised to notice that the truth didn't sound any different than a lie. "I'm the cook." She didn't mind talking to the man's legs. "I didn't even know Cindy was her daughter," she said, "if you can imagine that. I knew she was a Hanks and all. We line the kids up in alphabetical order, that's how they're in the computer. Hanks, Cindy. I knew her name was Hanks, but it never occurred to me that Cindy was related to my friend, Vernay."

The man suddenly pushed himself out from beneath the car. "What do you want?" he asked.

"I wanted to see if you need anything," she said, but that sounded vaguely sexual, so she added, "I wanted to see if there was anything I could do to help Cindy."

"Like what?" He wiped his hands on his pants and looked toward the house.

June stood up, and the man stood up too. She said she was sorry, that's all. She didn't look at him now that he was standing up. She didn't even know what she had imagined she might find. June had always trusted her instincts, but now she didn't.

A car drove by, going slow, the driver with his head turned toward them, looking.

"I read it in the paper yesterday." Yesterday's article had been brief, but today there were more details. She had been strangled with electrical cord. It said her body was found in the woods, on the edge of town. June had imagined Ralphie's garage, but that was wrong. She didn't want to think of the details, but she thought of them anyway, against her will. She thought of Vernay in the noisy truck with its mag wheels, sitting beside Ralphie's father. The paper described her body, and it told the things that had happened to her. There was no privacy for Vernay.

"I'm just sorry," she said again, and she turned to go. She walked to her car and opened the door. The little dog jumped into her car, and she yanked it back out. If it had been her instead of Vernay, Louise would have helped Bill. Her mother and brother would have flown in. If it had been her, the women from Bill's work would have crowded into her house with casseroles, and Louise would have had to fight them off. If it had been her, where would she be now?

She got inside, but he called after her.

She rolled her window down, and he came to her, but at first he didn't speak. He had one hand against her car, and he was leaning down toward her. She could smell machinery, oil and metal things, lubricants and fuel. She waited. Then he bent even closer and said, "If you ever would like to visit with Cindy . . . Well, she's got Mona and all, but Mona she's hurt her back right now." He hesitated. "Being's you asked." He stood up and looked at the house. "She's taking it hard," he said. He looked back at her, into her eyes, and June felt herself blush. "If you ever want to stop by and visit her, that'd be all right." He paused. "It's hard on her, but I guess it'll get easier."

"Sure," said June. She turned the key in the ignition, but the car didn't start the first time. She tried it again, and this time it worked.

"You know her from school, right? You a teacher or something?"

"I work in the cafeteria."

When he didn't say anything, June asked, "Does she have a father?"

But this was going too far. He leaned down, glaring into her eyes, so that she shrank back. "No!"

June forced herself to meet his gaze. "Are you going to keep her?"

She waited, but he didn't answer. He said, "It sounds like your starter switch might be going out. You ought to have that looked at."

She put her car in gear. "Anyway," she said, "I'll call you sometime." She drove off quickly.

It was nice that he thought of the child like that, as someone who needed things, a child who missed her mother, a child who was taking it hard. She hadn't expected that. At school they said the uncle worked at the salvage yard. They said there was incest in the family, but that was just a rumor.

June usually told Bill everything, but she wasn't sure how to explain her visit to the dead woman's brother. He thought she worried too much. She made mountains out of molehills, stuck her nose in things that weren't her business. He thought she got too wrapped up in the kids at work. He questioned her judgment. Bill was the kind of person who knew what he thought. He didn't second-guess himself. He had a point of view, and he believed in it, while June could always see things one way or another, which put her at a disadvantage.

It was kind of a lark, she would explain, if such a cheerful word could be used in such circumstances. It was an impulse, she would tell him. She felt oddly responsible, she'd say, not that it was her fault. But Vernay Hanks was dead, and she was not, and she felt an obligation. Obligation was the wrong word. She simply wanted to make sure the girl was safe. How could anyone argue with that? No, she'd have to say it wasn't enough to talk to her at school. She had to meet the uncle too.

There was incest in the family, she had heard. Surely he could understand her concern. People think, Let Children's Services take care of things, but anybody who works with children knew you couldn't rely on them. And even when Children's Services did respond, well, it wasn't like there were foster families lining up to help.

She wouldn't let Bill convince her that she was wrong to be concerned.

Chapter 3

S he got off the hook the first night. She arrived home late and Bill had already left for work. She wanted to tell him, but she wanted him to be on her side. She walked around the house, talking out loud. "It's just that I feel a certain obligation," she said. She gestured with her hand. He couldn't argue with how she felt. People feel the way they feel. She sat on the couch, looking at the empty chair where Bill would be sitting if he were home. "She's only ten years old."

He'd make an argument for Children's Services next. She had to keep in mind all her main points, and she counted them on her fingers. Obligation—but that wasn't exactly the right word—Children's Services, uncle . . . Bill didn't like children, and an appeal to our obligation toward the children of strangers would not fall on fertile ground.

June went to the phone and called her friend Louise. When Louise answered, she began to tell her about

Ralphie's father. She described seeing his picture in the paper that day, in the staff room. She told her what the assistant had said about incest. Louise didn't interrupt once except to make encouraging noises and appropriate comments like *for God's sake!* and *surely not!*

When she had finished, Louise asked the question that had been burning in June's mind: "What does it mean?" When June admitted that she didn't know, Louise said, "In some places, like maybe China or a place like that, maybe Thailand, I don't remember exactly, if you save someone's life, accidentally or not, then that person is indebted to you forever." Louise asked what the opposite of that would be: What if you were responsible for someone's death?

"I'm not exactly *responsible*," June said.

"And what about the poor daughter? At the very least, you have to try, in some small way, to make it up to her. Poor little lamb." Louise recently had had her first baby. "Do you know how traumatic it is for a child to lose its mother? A child never gets over that, I'll tell you. And a *girl*—that's even worse. Just wait until she hits puberty. She might repress it all now, and everybody thinks she's made it, but just wait. I'm telling you, she's a time bomb."

June thought this time bomb idea was off the mark, but she didn't want an argument. Now she told Louise about her visit to the uncle. She told her everything she could remember about it. She was good with details. She mentioned the Chihuahua who had come out from beneath the front porch and the plastic Santa across the street.

June felt relieved and vindicated when Louise acted like it was perfectly normal that a person in June's situation would visit the home of the murdered woman's brother, pretending to be a friend of the victim. Even more important, she seemed to have no doubt about the purpose of such a visit: to see that Cindy was safe. Who else was there to look after her?

"The main thing," said June, "is what's best for Cindy."

"What about her father?" asked Louise.

"There isn't a father." She hated that phrase—it seemed to let men off the hook entirely—but it was efficient, and she used it.

"Poor little lamb," said Louise, again. She had never met Cindy and so she could imagine her in this way, small, helpless, and innocent.

"The least I can do is make sure she's safe."

"Absolutely."

June could hear the baby fussing in the background, and she knew the conversation was coming to an end.

"It *is* dishonest," June said.

"But if you were that poor mother, wouldn't you want people looking out for your child? Believe me, if you were a mother, that's all you'd care about."

June didn't like it when Louise implied that the way June cared about children was less than the way mothers cared about them, but it was a small point, maybe, and anyway, Louise's attention had shifted away from her. The baby was crying now, and she had to go.

June lay awake that night until she heard Bill open the front door. She listened while he played music in the living room. She imagined him sitting in his chair, smoking. She could smell the cigarette. He would be drinking a whisky. Sometimes she'd get up and go sit with him, but that night she lay in bed and waited. It wasn't like she was going to carry on a long relationship with the Hankses, she would tell him. In a couple months it would be summer, and school would be out.

After the music stopped, she could hear him in the shower. When he finally came to bed and lay on his back next to her, June slid her arm over him and began to talk, but before she could even get to the part where she visited Mr. Hanks and impersonated his dead sister's friend, he said, "Oh, for God's sake, June!" He said, "Vernay Hanks doesn't have anything to do with you." He said, "Just forget about it!"

June was quiet. People with children have to remind each other not to talk loud. If they have a baby, like Louise, they don't want it to start crying, but June and Bill didn't have that problem. They could make as much noise as they wanted.

Despite this, when Bill talked again he used a quiet voice, same as you'd use if there was a baby in the next room, a mild whispering voice. "You're always getting involved in other people's business. You're turning into an old lady! You know that?" And then he repeated, "It doesn't have anything to do with you. For God's sake, June."

He didn't expect an answer, and she didn't give him one.

Then, because Bill could sleep anytime, no matter what—he could sleep through the worst crises, it didn't matter—he rolled to his side and slept.

Chapter 4

On Sunday June drove to the Hankses' house. She parked her car and got out. It was April, but it was a warm, sunny day. She had a jacket on, and she unbuttoned it. The window and front door were open; she could see the screen door as she approached, but she couldn't see inside the house. She knocked on the door and then turned, glancing at the house across the street to see if the Santa was still there, and it was. There was an American flag too, flying from the front porch. June hadn't noticed that before.

"Yeah?"

June turned back around. "It's me," she said through the screen.

The man hesitated and then remembered. "Oh, right, the lady from school." June was annoyed. Usually if men saw her once, they didn't forget who she was.

He opened the door, but he didn't invite her in, and he didn't introduce himself. He stepped outside. He was shirtless, and she looked away. "You came to see Cindy?"

"Yeah," she said in a tone that let him know what a stupid question it was. But instead of calling for Cindy or introducing himself or inviting her in, the uncle just stood looking at her. June looked back, but after a while she felt funny about it. "I didn't get your name, when I was here before." It was up to him to say these things, but if he wasn't going to, if he didn't know basic manners like saying my name is so-and-so, then she was just going to have to do everything. "My name is June Duvall."

"I thought you'd call first," he said, which was not exactly the appreciative response you'd expect for the friend of your dead sister. But then he opened the door and said, "Come on in." He led the way. "Cindy!" he yelled.

June stepped inside. Usually when men have a house with no woman to take care of it, things go to hell, but nothing had gone to hell in here. The room was small and crowded, but it was fairly neat. There was an old plaid couch and two stuffed chairs to sit on. There was a coffee table and a TV set. June wondered fleetingly if most of the kids at school lived in houses like this, neat and purposeful, with the windows open and fresh air blowing in. She had imagined something altogether different. At least, she had imagined a house messier than her own. Don't children make a mess? Don't they get everything out and leave it, make everything dirty and not clean it, throw things around or break them? That's what people said.

June and the man stood in the small room facing each other. She looked at his hands, his face, at his eyes, his mouth, his chest, and then away.

"You got a name?" June asked, and he looked surprised, like he hadn't noticed the fact that he'd neglected his half of the introduction ceremony.

"Harlan," he said. He looked around at the house, and it struck June that this was a place where outsiders came, police, social workers, child-welfare workers. Poor people didn't get privacy, she thought. At school they didn't bat an eye when they had to fill out papers with questions about their income and who lived at their house. They were used to people discussing their parenting, talking about their family fights, asking if anyone had been sexually abused, who slept where, if they drank or used drugs, if they had lice, if they were mentally unstable, if they spanked their kids or yelled at them, if they bought cable TV and sent their children to school without coats. It was all for the record. They were poor, and their business was everybody's business. There were experts who could help them, or, anyway, *document* their problems.

"How do you know her?" Harlan asked.

"From school, like I said. I work in the kitchen at her school."

"My sister, I mean. How do you know Vernay?"

"Oh," June said. "Well." She licked her lips. "I'm not even sure where I first met her, but I guess we used to see each other at the restaurant some."

"She trusted everybody. That was her problem," said Harlan.

"What a loss," said June, but Harlan Hanks wasn't paying attention to her anymore because Cindy had appeared.

Whenever she saw the kids outside of school, June was always surprised at how small they were. In school third graders seemed like average-size adults, and by the time they got to fifth grade June had the impression that they were bigger than she was, although clearly that was not true.

Cindy was one of the bigger kids, but she was still much smaller than June. She was a fifth grader, a long-legged, loud girl, full of false bravado, a girl who pushed in the lunch line. She was not a poor little lamb. Cindy had wild curly hair. She had her uncle's high cheekbones, like an Indian, and his confidence. She was a girl who seemed self-contained, a girl who knew herself and didn't worry about what everybody else thought. She stood in front of June with the fat, bug-eyed Chihuahua in her arms. She didn't look like a girl facing a dire and uncertain future, but looks can fool you, June thought. At school Cindy was a leader. The other kids looked up to her. She was like Bill. She knew what she wanted. She knew what she thought. She never hesitated in the lunch line, and no one shoved her. She got in fights sometimes. She had been suspended more than once. The year before, she had convinced some of the other girls that she could control the weather. June would hear them in the lunch line, begging her, *Please bring back the sun, Cindy!* At school she was powerful, but here she was just a girl holding a Chihuahua.

"You look like my mom," she said, but before June could respond, she changed the subject. She said that besides the dog, she also had a gerbil named Marge. She had a fish and a bird. She wanted a palomino stallion, but she didn't have one of those yet. She had two cats, she said, but they were wild and lived in a vacant lot down the street.

Cindy didn't want to take a walk. She didn't want to go to the park or get ice cream. They sat on her front porch steps, and the Chihuahua named Little Babe sat beside them. Cindy had a notebook on her lap and as they talked she drew pictures.

"I used to love horses when I was a girl too," said June.

"But now you don't?" asked the girl, and then she added, "Horses are my favorite animal." And she drew a picture of a horse with a long, flowing tail.

"Mine are elephants and turtles."

"You can only have one."

"Elephants, then."

"If you could be any animal, what would you be?" asked Cindy. "But don't say bird. Everybody says bird all the time. If you could be any animal but a bird, what would you be?"

June hadn't thought of this for a while, and now she hesitated. She used to think gazelle, but she'd hate to be chased and then grabbed by the neck, thrown to the ground, and eaten. The world is a violent place, thought June. Birth is violent, death is violent, and in between it's violent too.

"If you could be any animal, but you had to decide in ten seconds, what would it be?"

"Tiger," said June.

"My mom used to say you could tell about somebody from what animal they picked."

"What animal did she pick?"

"Deer."

It got cooler out and June wrapped her coat around her. She pulled her collar up to keep her neck warm. Her neck was always cold. "White-tailed deer?" she asked.

Cindy frowned. "Yeah," she said, but then she shook her head. "A deer is a deer, you know."

She drew a picture of a deer, and then she drew a guitar and hearts.

"My mom loved music, and she loved dancing. She loved singing, and so do I. I love singing and dancing and art. I love all kinds of animals, and I love insects. I love praying mantises. They actually do look like they're praying, you know," Cindy said. "If you see one on a rock in the sun, it looks like it's praying for food and then a bug comes by and the praying mantis catches it." She paused and then continued, "A praying mantis lays its eggs in a sac, and when the sac opens, so many tiny praying mantises come out, but you can't touch them. Even the slightest touch of a human hand can kill a baby praying mantis. They are so delicate."

She drew a cross and began coloring it in. Suddenly she turned to June. "Just between you and me," she said, "I'm not sure there is a Heaven."

June didn't say anything. She picked up the little dog and petted it. She wished she could think of something important and comforting, yet honest, to say but she couldn't.

Cindy began to sing as she drew. She sang, "We'll all miss you now that you're gone." She suddenly set her notebook down. "I don't know why we can't sing. Everybody just wants to mope. That's all Uncle Harlan has done since it happened."

"Your uncle seems nice," said June.

But Cindy changed the subject. "My father is Mexican," she said.

"Mexican? Really?"

"Didn't she ever tell you that?"

June thought she had five seconds to answer that question, and the best she could come up with in that time was, "No, she never did." Which was the truth. June had never told a long, complicated lie before, but she had heard that the best thing was to stick to the truth as much as possible.

"Where does your father live?" asked June.

"Maybe Mexico," Cindy said, and then she added, "My grandmother knows."

"Why don't you ask her?"

But Cindy didn't answer the question. "She says Harry Potter is the devil."

Some girls and a few of the smaller boys would take your hand, but Cindy wasn't that kind of little girl. Some of the sexually abused ones would get too close, would stand right next to you, touching all the time, like they didn't know about the idea of being too close, but Cindy didn't do that either.

"Do you like living with your uncle?"

"It's okay."

June heard Harlan behind them. She didn't turn, but she

knew he was standing at the screen door. She could feel his eyes on her. She didn't know if he had heard her question or not.

"He seems nice," June added.

There was a jump rope lying on the sidewalk, and Cindy picked it up and began to jump. While she jumped, she asked, "Do you go to church?"

But June didn't want to talk about religion.

"I go to Thursday Club, that's every Thursday, and I learn about Jesus. It's Thursday Club, for kids." Cindy was still jumping. She wasn't doing hot potatoes though. She was jumping slowly, one leg and then the other, like skipping. "Are you Christian?"

"No." You weren't supposed to talk about religion to the kids or tell them that you didn't believe in the war or anything important like that, but June supposed it was all right to respond to a direct question.

"At Thursday Club they say the world is three thousand years old, but Uncle Harlan says that's bullshit."

June knew she should tell Cindy not to say the word *bullshit,* but instead she laughed. She hoped Harlan was still there behind her. She had long hair, and she tossed it.

Cindy added, "They say sinners will burn forever, but I don't believe it."

"Why do you go?"

"To Thursday Club? Uncle Harlan thinks I need a mother figure."

"A mother figure?"

"Mrs. Shoemaker—she teaches Bible class. He was worried about a mother figure even before my mother"—she said the word quietly—"died."

June turned around and saw that Harlan was gone. "What about your grandmother?"

"Uncle Harlan hates her!" Cindy exclaimed.

"He hates your grandmother?"

"And so did Vernay."

"Why do you call your mother Vernay?"

"That's her name, isn't it?" Cindy began to jump faster. "Anyhow, they give us coats and shoes, and once they took us to see horses." She turned all the way around as she jumped. When she faced June again, she added, "Vernay thought they were nosy!"

Before June could explore this interesting turn in the conversation, Cindy began to chant in rhythm with her jumps.

> *Cinder-ella dressed in yell-a*
> *Went upstairs to kiss her fell-a*
> *Made a mistake*
> *And kissed a snake*

A sexual rhyme, but the girls who recited it didn't seem to know.

> *How many babies did she make?*

And she began counting as she jumped. One, two, three, four—and on and on, endless babies, that fertile Cinderella.

Thirty-three, thirty-four, there was no end in sight—when suddenly Cindy stopped. She threw down the jump rope and came to stand in front of June. "Why didn't you come to her service?"

"Oh," said June. She hadn't planned this out. "I didn't know about it. I'm sorry. I had lost touch with your mom, a little bit."

"You mean you used to be friends with her, and then you weren't?"

"No. I just mean I hadn't seen her for a while."

"Did you still like her?"

"Of course I did."

"Do you have people that you like and then you don't like them?"

"No," June said. "Hardly ever."

"People always change their minds about things."

"Not when they love someone."

"Did you love my mom?"

June stood up. She should never have come here.

"Do you think she would care if I changed my name to my father's name?" Cindy asked.

"Your last name?"

"Yeah, instead of Hanks like handkerchief."

"What was his name?"

"Hernandez."

"Cindy Hernandez, that sounds nice."

"Or maybe it was Fernandez."

Chapter 5

The police came over on Monday afternoon. They rang the bell, and Bill asked them to step inside. He was dressed in his black chef's pants and his white shirt, and they were dressed in their blue uniforms. They stood inside the front door. They didn't have a search warrant, and he wasn't obligated to let them in, but it seemed like the polite thing to do, June could see. They just had a couple of questions. They were chasing things down, they said once, and another time they called it *tying things up*.

She didn't like them being in the house, but there was nothing illegal sitting around. There might be pot someplace, but it was out of sight. If the police saw something illegal in the normal course of a visit, they didn't need a search warrant to arrest you, June knew, and with this thought she turned to glance around the living room.

The men asked June to tell them about her encounter with Ronald Pruett on the afternoon of March 23. She said she had just gotten off work. She said there was a staff meeting at school, so she had worked late. "I was driving home on Jackson Street when my fuel pump went out." She told about Ralphie's father stopping to help.

It was time for Bill to leave for work, but he stood in the entryway, close to her, and she was glad he was there. She wondered if people committed murder sometimes because it made them more interesting and important; made people want to know things about them; made them special. June used to think of murder as something shocking and extraordinary, but lately she had been struck by the banality of it.

She wondered if the police were thinking about the fact that she might have been the victim instead of Vernay Hanks. Were they thinking what a shame it wasn't her, a woman with no children?

"Do you have any children?" they asked, and Bill said no.

She wondered how being a cop affected the way a person saw things. She thought of the criminals and wondered if they were ever sorry later. Maybe people eventually understand what they've done and are sorry, but then it's too late. You can't take it back. You have to live with it. She hoped so. If only people were sorry later, truly sorry—not sorry but it was your fault too, or sorry it was because of my parents—although, June knew as well as anyone, it often was. If only people were genuinely sorry, she felt that she could forgive them for anything. Even the people who killed their neighbors with machetes, even the politicians who sat around twiddling their thumbs while it happened, she could forgive them all, if only there was honest regret. There was not enough regret in the world, June thought that day standing in the entryway of her house with the two cops and Bill who was going to be late for work, if he wasn't careful.

Joe Friday had his little notebook, and he wrote things down as she spoke. On TV Joe Friday seemed old, but this guy didn't. He seemed like somebody ahead of you a couple grades in school, someone nobody liked, and now he was a cop with a gun and a little notebook, and if he saw something illegal lying on your table, even if it was just a bag of pot, he could arrest you.

"Had you ever noticed the suspect following you?"

"No."

The other officer took a photograph out of his pocket and handed it to Bill. June leaned over to see that it was a picture of Pruett's blue truck with its beige fender and mag wheels. "Have you ever seen this truck in your neighborhood?"

Bill handed it back. To his knowledge, he'd never seen that vehicle before. If he had, he didn't remember it. *To my knowledge,* he had said. It was the way you talked to people like cops.

Cindy had told June that she looked like Vernay, and now June imagined the woman in the paper. Usually they showed the same photograph, a picture of the dead woman alive and smiling at the camera. June hated to have her picture taken, but Vernay seemed completely at ease in front of the camera. Some poor people have bad teeth, but hers were nice. It was funny that even though June had seen her in person at school, when she thought of her, she thought of the black-and-white photograph in the newspaper.

June couldn't tell if they looked alike or not. They both wore their hair long. They both had brown hair and dark eyes. They both had wide faces, dark eyebrows, and large mouths. They could have been sisters, she supposed.

She had heard of killers who went for a certain look, but what did it mean? Did they have a certain type? People have types. She had a type and it was Bill. Italians were her type, maybe, or dark guys anyway. Mexicans, men from Chile and El Salvador, Greeks, French guys, Black Irish. Did murderers have one type they dated and another type they killed? Did they look for someone like their mother?

The cops were getting ready to leave. The man with the little notebook flipped it shut and put it in his pocket.

June wasn't ready for them to go. She had questions of her own, but she wasn't sure she was allowed to ask them. She wanted to know what they thought of this. Who was Ronald Pruett, and would he have gone on killing other women, or had he gotten it out of his system? Do people who kill try it once and then move on to other things, take up a hobby, get a second job, join a softball team, and just get too dang busy to murder anyone? It must take a lot of time and effort. How is it that people who show so little initiative in other ways become murderers? And, most important, what did killers make of what they had done, later? What story did they tell themselves? And how did they manage to keep it a secret? Wouldn't they eventually tell their best friend or their wife or, in an impulsive moment, someone in a bar or at a party? Wouldn't they tell somebody sometime? Wouldn't what they had done linger in the air around them? Wouldn't people sense it? But no, she reminded herself, she had stood next to Pruett, and she hadn't noticed anything. Maybe that was the most disturbing part of it. We are sealed off from each other, June thought. We only know what someone else lets us know. We are alone, with so little to go on.

"I guess he was arrested before," said June, but the cops didn't answer her. She turned to Joe Friday. "The papers said domestic violence," she reminded him. "And one time he beat up a woman in a bar." She could feel Bill giving her a look, but she kept her eyes on the cops. They were leaving now. They were not going to indulge in chitchat with the public. They had jobs to do. They would save conversation until they got to the car. Maybe Joe Friday would say it was too bad Pruett hadn't killed this one instead, so poor little Cindy Hanks would still have a mother.

Chapter 6

Mikey Black had begun to start fires. Soon he would be sent to a care facility in Portland and they would never see him again, but today he was in the kitchen with June and Missy, serving pizza medallions and popcorn chicken.

It was May, and a group of children in Iraq had just been killed. One boy had been flying a kite when he was suddenly dismembered by a cluster bomb. June kept thinking of him. She kept thinking of his mother, who would surely be saying, "If only I'd kept him home that day. If only I'd been with him. If only I hadn't given him that kite but had chosen a soccer ball instead."

Somebody sits around in a lab designing things like cluster bombs that come apart on impact and tear people's limbs off, June thought. Somebody figures this out. And then he goes home at night and plays with his children. He eats and laughs and is a human being. If an entire country can rationalize cluster bombs, then why shouldn't a man be able to rationalize his own, private murders? The president could be a hero for launching a bombing campaign that flattened cities, but if a little boy started a fire in his mother's closet he was locked up.

"But what about your mother?" asked Missy. Missy's own mother was in jail. "Why can't you stay with your mother?" She drew out the word *mother,* so it had about nine syllables and her voice went up and then down at the end. "Why can't you?" The fact that she herself was being raised by an aunt didn't seem to occur to Missy.

They could hear the first class coming. The classes came in through the gym. The sound of their feet echoed, and the wide open space made them want to run and fan out, so that the teachers kept reminding them, *Stay in line, slow down!*

"My mother can't take care of me," said Mikey.

"Don't go to foster care!" cried Missy. "They make you work all the time! I've heard about that. They make you scrub floors and work all the time."

But Mikey said, "Sometimes they have ponies," and Missy was quiet, thinking of this.

They were lined up in their places, ready to hand out plates of pepperoni pizza, popcorn chicken, or the vegetarian selection, peanut butter and jelly on white bread.

"People become foster parents because they love children," said June. Lie, lie, lie, she thought, but sometimes we simply must lie, there is no getting around it.

"I might go to foster care," said Missy.

"You are not!" Mikey exclaimed.

Missy was a girl who couldn't hide her need for

approval, and the kids resented her for it. They all wanted friends, but they pretended not to. They wanted to be smart and well-liked, to be picked first for games, to be like other people, to have children in the lunchroom call, *Sit here!* They all wanted these things, but they pretended indifference, and they resented someone like Missy, who was so naked in her own need. They ran from her on the playground, pushed her in the lunch line, and bullied her after school. "You live with your aunt and she doesn't believe in Christmas," Mikey added.

This was always a danger for the kids—that they might end up in the custody of Jehovah's Witnesses and no longer be allowed to celebrate birthdays or Christmas.

"She has a dog!" Missy said, in her aunt's defense.

Mikey was not going to foster care anyway. He was going to a psych ward, and the children there hardly ever got out, June had been told. By the time they went there, they were lost to the world.

She put her hand on Mikey's back. He had a little back, and spread out, her fingers covered most of it. She wanted to hold the children. She wanted to set them in her lap and fold her arms around them, but you couldn't do that. You could touch the arm or pat their back a little, you could hug them, if you were female, but you had to keep a guard. What do we know about each other? she wondered. Everybody knew Mikey was troubled, but there were other things about him too, wonderful sweet things, harder to get at, harder to express, and he mostly kept those to himself.

$\bullet \quad \bullet \quad \bullet$

The next day, Cindy joined the lunchroom helpers.

The kids came through the line, and they were handed their food. Nothing eventful happened until Buddy Knowles asked Cindy why she wasn't in Mexico. "I thought you were going to Mexico," he said, taunting her. "I thought you were going on the Greyhound bus, like what you said." Buddy was one of the bigger boys, a fifth grader. He had a father in prison and a mother in Iraq. He turned to the kids in back of him, Freddy, José Miguel, Victor, Desiree, and Ashley, and said, "See! I told you she wasn't taking no Greyhound bus."

But Cindy said she was too. She said she knew how.

Buddy said, "I bet you never even been on a Greyhound bus," while June said to move on, keep moving.

Cindy said, "I bet you never even *seen* one." And then she shouted, "Anyhow your mamma is too fat to even fit on a Greyhound bus!"

"Your mamma is dead!" he shouted back, and the kids knew he had gone too far.

The only one oblivious to this was Freddy, and he took advantage of the moment of stunned silence to announce, "I am going to Mexico. I'm going to Mexico to visit my family. They are Mexicans, from Mexico."

The children forgot the horrible thing about Cindy's mother. They said, "Oh, get out of here, Freddy. Fat Freddy, Freckled Freddy, Fruity Freddy." Freddy was a skinny little boy but they didn't care, they liked alliteration.

"Hey!" shouted June. She pointed a long wooden spoon at Buddy. He was the ringleader. "I don't want that kind of talk!" she said to him. It was good to single somebody out. "Now move on!"

"He ain't Mexican," muttered Cindy.

And Missy, wanting to get on Cindy's good side, added, "He's too stupid to be Mexican."

But June said that was enough, and they finished working with no more outbursts.

Every day there was news about Vernay, or something about Ralphie's father. Ralphie hadn't come back to school. He had gone, they said, to Salem, to live with his grandmother.

June wondered what it would be like to be the mother of someone who raped and murdered women. Would you look back at ten thousand things you had done while he was growing up, hateful things that might have gotten into him and then grown into a murderous rage? Would you think, If only you had been different. If only you had read him poetry or taken him to the movies, or shown him what a woman is—the beautiful sweet part, the tender heart, the soft hands, the dreams, the humanity. If he had known about the humanity, he wouldn't have done it, would he?

One day, after Bill left for work, June drove to the Hankses' house. She hadn't meant to go back there again. She had told herself not to. Vernay's family wasn't her business. Even though she had almost begun to believe her own lie, the truth was that she had never even met Vernay. Louise said she had to make sure about the uncle. "This is what happens to girls," Louise said, "while everybody stands around saying it's not their business." But Louise had never met Harlan, and so she could have those thoughts.

June thought of him standing behind her while she sat on the steps with Cindy. She hadn't turned to see him, but she knew he was there. She thought of him watching, his face pressed against the screen door.

She hadn't planned to go back, but Harlan didn't seem surprised to see her. She stepped inside the doorway and stood, nervously.

"Sit down, sit down," Harlan said, and she sat. The house was just as clean as it had been the day of her other visit. The living room was small, and she sat on the couch, while he stood across the room, facing her.

Louise said that if June hadn't been able to tell about Pruett, then how could her instincts be trusted when it came to Harlan Hanks? June knew the signs of sex abuse to look for in children, but it was like reading the signs of alcoholism, or suicide. The signs were all around. And what if there was abuse? Then what? It wasn't like you pick up the phone and tell someone and they fix it.

Harlan was saying that his sister's personal things were still in her room. "We didn't clean it out yet," he said. "We thought Mona would do it, but she hurt her back. She hasn't been able to get out of bed for nearly a week now."

He nodded toward the hallway. "Cindy used to share the room with Vernay. They got the two beds in there. But she can't sleep in there because of all her mother's things."

Cindy had come into the room now, with the dog waddling at her heels.

"Cindy's a brave girl," he said now, for her benefit, "but she don't like all those things of her mother's everywhere. Tell her, Cindy." When Cindy didn't tell her, he continued, "So we were thinking, me and Cindy were, that if you didn't mind maybe you'd be willing to go into the room and take some of the things."

Things, he kept calling them, which wasn't very specific, June thought. He said they needed to box up whatever they weren't keeping and get rid of it, but Cindy said "No!" in a loud voice, which made Little Babe begin barking.

"Shut up!" Harlan yelled at the dog, which was something the school tried very hard to get the kids to stop saying. It would be nice, June reflected, to think the kids learned this phrase through listening to their parents' conversations with dogs, but she doubted it. "Okay, okay," he said to Cindy. June knew then, from his voice and from the way he looked at Cindy, that he was one of those people who treated kids like they knew just as much as adults, which was always a mistake, regardless of what the anarchists might say. They are children, and they need us to tell them things, June thought. She hoped that, in other ways, Harlan did know the difference between children and adults.

"We'll keep whatever you want to keep, little lady. Just relax." At any rate, Harlan said, June should take the clothes.

"Take the clothes?" June's hand went to her heart and sat there, palm open.

"She's the same size as Vernay, don't you think so, Cindy?"

But Cindy was not going to be dragged into this part of the conversation.

"I wouldn't feel right, taking her clothes," June said, and then she waited, but Harlan just stood looking at her. "Surely she must have a friend, a close friend, or a sister or someone like that—"

"Mona said she'd do it!" cried Cindy.

"Mona's back is out. You know that."

Cindy crossed her arms in front of her chest. She wore a yellow jumper that was too small for her, and she was barefoot. Her hair needed a good brushing. Presumably Mona would tend to these details once she was on her feet again.

"Tell her, Cindy. You can't sleep in there with all your mom's stuff. That's what you said."

Cindy admitted it was true.

"They look like monsters in the dark," Harlan explained. "They look like witches and alligators." He turned to Cindy. "Tell her, Cindy. You say even with the closet door shut they are like monsters."

"There are no monsters. Everybody knows that," Cindy said.

"Yes, but they make you think of monsters," he insisted. "Even with the closet door shut, even with the night-light on, with your bedroom door open—" He glanced at June with what appeared to be the hope for approval. "Even with me in the next room and Little Babe and your gerbil—"

"And the statue of Baby Jesus," added Cindy.

"You'll feel better when the room is cleaned out, is all

I'm saying." He turned to June now. "I always come in and turn on the light to show her it's just the same in the dark as it is in the light, only difference is we can't see."

June hesitated, thinking of what he had said. *The only difference is we can't see.* It seemed to imply a philosophical bent to his thinking, but surely that wasn't right. Harlan was a simple man. He was not a thinker. He was not a man with an original mind. He was not sensitive. If he was sensitive, she thought, he would understand that she didn't want Vernay's things, whatever they were. She didn't want to see Vernay's bed. She didn't want to look in her closet. She didn't want to touch her clothes.

"You asked if there was anything you could do," Harlan reminded her.

And so June found herself walking down the hallway to Vernay Hanks' bedroom with an empty box in each hand. When she got to the door, she turned to look at Harlan and Cindy, standing in the living room at the end of the hall, watching her. Harlan nodded encouragingly, and she turned and opened the door. The curtains were pulled shut and the blinds drawn so it was dark. She felt the wall and flipped a light switch, which turned on a lamp.

There were two single mattresses set on the floor on box springs, one against one wall and one against another. One of them had Barbie-doll sheets and pillowcases. A Barbie pillow was strewn on the floor, and June picked it up. She went to the other bed, Vernay's, and sat down. The cover was a thin ivory-colored cotton blanket, and on the pillow sat a white stuffed cat. There was a little table next to the bed; in addition to the lamp, it held an ashtray, an ink pen, hand cream, one gold hoop earring, a book of crossword puzzles, and a travel book, *Let's Go Mexico,* which seemed designed for middle-class college students. The book was open facedown, which anybody knows, June thought, can ruin a book's spine. The table had a little drawer, and June slid it open. Inside she found a pack of matches, stationery, and an emery board. She shut the drawer and sat on the bed, looking around. The walls were painted pink and the baseboards white. It was a calm room. June ran her hand over the pillow. A week ago Vernay Hanks was alive, sitting here, in this room, thought June. She picked up the stuffed cat and held it in her lap. A little breeze blew in the window. There was a dresser against the wall. There was a closet with two doors that opened up.

She shut her eyes and told herself to relax. There was nothing hard about filling up boxes with dresses, she told herself. If she had died, Louise would be the one to empty her closets and her drawers. If she had died, Bill would be so sad, she thought, and she imagined Bill being told, Bill not believing, Bill walking through their room looking at her things, sitting on their bed. *Poor Bill,* they would all say, *he was so in love with her. Poor Bill, he'll never find another woman like that.*

She set the cat on the bed and went to the dresser. She didn't know if other people had such stupid thoughts or if it was just her.

The top drawer was for underwear. All the underwear was in neat piles, the underpants in one pile, bras in another, stockings in the corner, and one white slip. The second drawer was full of pants; blue jeans and slacks. The third drawer had sweaters.

There was a free place downtown. You could donate your clothes or bedding, old towels, appliances, books, or toys. June told herself she'd take the clothes there, but then it occurred to her that some of the families at Washington Elementary used the free store. Maybe some Washington mother would get Vernay's clothes. Maybe every time that woman came to pick up her child, Cindy would see her mother's shiny black pants, her mother's red sweater, or shoes.

"Find anything you want?"

June jumped and looked up at Cindy, standing in the doorway with a box of plastic garbage bags in her hand. Cindy came into the room and sat on Vernay's bed with her feet on the floor. If she felt uncomfortable about June going through her mother's room, she didn't show it.

"She was going to take me to Mexico." Cindy picked up the book from beside the bed, *Let's Go Mexico.* "Barra de Navidad," she read from the book. "See, we were gonna go there."

It occurred to June that she had better hurry up. She had been gone too long already and, even though Bill wasn't home, he might call. And then either she would have to lie, and she had never lied to him before, or she would have to tell the truth, which was getting more and more complicated all the time. She wondered if this was how lies began, as complications that got too big to explain, so that a lie became almost as honest as any truth you could think to tell.

"Navidad, that's like birthday," Cindy said.

June pulled the underwear drawer open and emptied it into one of the plastic bags. She did the same with the other drawers. When she had filled up a bag, she dragged it to the doorway.

"Don't you want any of it?" asked Cindy.

June opened the closet. It was full of dresses and blouses, jackets, sweaters, high boots, dressy heels, and work pumps. It didn't seem right that someone's accessories should last longer than their body.

"Size eight," said Cindy, who was now lying on the bed. "What size do you wear? Take some of them! Go ahead. She'd want you to have them." And then she added, "Those shiny black ones are her dancing shoes."

"Don't you have an aunt or something?" asked June, but even as she protested, she slipped on a pair of the shoes.

"Try the dancing ones," suggested Cindy, sitting up.

They were shiny black shoes with long, pointed toes and high heels.

"Harlan will just give them to Goodwill." Cindy slipped her own small feet into a pair of red shoes. She stood up and walked across the floor. "You know they'll just throw everything into bins for people to dig through. Maybe they lose one of the shoes and they don't even care because they got so many." She slipped off the shoes and pushed them toward June. "Go ahead," she said, "she'd want you to take them."

June began to make a pile for herself. They kept saying

she should, and why not? She chose the dancing shoes, a pair of red high heels, and a pair of tall black boots. She put some lacy blouses in the pile and two dresses. She chose a pretty blue scarf. She stuffed the rest of the things in bags, filled up the boxes with everything that sat around on the table and on the floor. She left the book about Mexico.

"Where have you been sleeping, if you can't sleep in here?" she asked.

"On the couch."

June looked at Cindy, lying on her mother's bed.

"Mona didn't like my mom, and my mom didn't like her neither," Cindy said. "Mona said my mom was a bad mom, but my mom said Mona wasn't even a mom at all, and she didn't know what she was talking about, and Mona said she was too a mom only the dad had the kids, and my mom said, oh that's right—I forgot all about that."

"Who's Mona?"

"Nobody." Cindy turned and buried her face in the pillow, but she wasn't crying.

June thought of the pillow, still smelling like Vernay, and she asked Cindy for fresh sheets and pillowcases. When the girl got up, she stripped both beds. She would need to dust and sweep. She picked up a yellow skirt from the floor and held it up. It was linen, a nice fabric, an expensive cut, and it was her size. Maybe it was one of the last things Vernay had worn before she was killed. June put it in the pile of things she was keeping. She didn't know how she would explain these new clothes to Bill. She'd have to tell him the whole story; otherwise, she was weaving a tangled web, and that was not the kind of marriage they had. It was funny how some things seemed reasonable while they were being lived, more or less. One thing led to another in a logical way, but those same things, spoken, appeared utterly outlandish. June noticed a lacy yellow bra under the little table, and she picked it up and put it in her box too. She would wash everything first. Anyway, it was not so different than going to the Goodwill.

When Cindy came back with the sheets and the cleaning things, June said, "You go on. I'll do this."

But Cindy didn't go on. She lay down on her mother's bed with her hands behind her head. "When was the last time you saw her?" she asked.

"I can't even remember," said June quickly.

"We were going to go to the beach. She was going to get off work, and we were going over there for the whole weekend, and maybe longer."

Vernay had been killed at the beginning of spring break. She was killed on that first Friday, after school, when the flowers bloomed and the days stretched ahead, full of possibility. There was a staff meeting after school, and everyone complained. The kids had gone home, shouting and running, but the adults had stayed behind in the library. The principal passed around chocolate, but that didn't placate anybody. And then June's car had broken down, but she didn't want a ride. It was funny, June thought, the way we have our separate lives, and then they intersect. She went to the window and looked out. Across the street, the dog barked.

"Those ladies at work were always jealous of her, everywhere she worked they were. It was because she was so pretty. And they were just mean, because they weren't pretty, and they wanted to be. She could have been a movie star, that's what I thought, if she wanted, but she didn't want to. And we were going to get a motel, a real motel with a swimming pool. We were going to get a motel that took dogs too, so Little Babe could come. And then she didn't come home." Cindy rolled from her back to her stomach. "I don't know why some people don't like dogs."

She was probably supposed to help Cindy identify her feelings right now, but June didn't say anything.

"We just thought she was off somewheres."

June left the window and went to sit on the bed where Cindy was lying.

"When she didn't come home, my Uncle Harlan, he said, oh she's just off somewheres. And I just waited the whole time."

June wondered if this was the part where she was supposed to put her hand on Cindy's back and say *There, there, it will be all right.* We always say that, *it will be all right,* but it's just not true. Sometimes it's not all right, she thought.

"She was fighting with her boyfriend," added Cindy.

"She had a boyfriend?"

Cindy turned her head to look at June now, and she frowned. "Course she had a boyfriend. She always had a boyfriend."

"She was so pretty," offered June.

"One time The Bruiser, you know The Bruiser, from TV,

the wrestler, he kissed her cheek. She was at a wrestling match of his, and he took one look at her, and he came out in the audience where she was sitting, and he kissed her on the cheek. I told her, never wash that cheek again, but she said she had to."

When she left the Hankses' house that day, June drove straight to the free store. There was a collection bin out front, and she dropped the bags and boxes into it and drove home. Maybe later Vernay's clothes would show up in the halls of George Washington Elementary School, but she couldn't worry about that. She had cleaned the bedroom. The bed was made with fresh sheets. She had polished the mirror, dusted, and swept the floor. All of Cindy's mother's clothes were gone.

When June got home, she put away the things she had kept for herself. She had planned to wash them, but then she didn't. Clothes have a smell on them. Not a bad smell and maybe too mild to be called a smell at all, a scent. A scent that is not just laundry soap but perfume, shampoo, the food someone has eaten, the rooms they've moved through, the people they've seen, who they've made love with, the oils from their body. She held the lace bra to her face and shut her eyes. She thought of Vernay, who was dead. She thought of all the things that make up a person, and then those things are gone. She put the bra in her dresser and thought she would wash it later. She thought,

At some point a person disappears from the earth, but Vernay hasn't disappeared yet.

Later that night, Bill called. Bill was a romantic. He called from McMurray's, the front desk, and he whispered. He couldn't wait to get home. *Baby,* he called her. All the time, *baby.* He was a big, lusty man, a sexy man, a wild, sweet, loud, voracious, sensual man. He was different from anybody else. She shut her eyes and imagined him alone whispering into the phone, with his white chef's apron, his white hat, his dark lips, his legs pressed against the front desk.

Chapter 7

The following day, she put on Vernay's red high heels and went to Darrel's Hamburgers on Ninth Street, to meet Louise. Louise was already there, in a booth, with the baby. Before the baby, the two women had seen each other frequently. They were both southerners: June from South Carolina and Louise a Georgian. They had the same sense of humor and the same interest in human drama, which their husbands sometimes mistook for gossip. They liked the same things, objected to the same things, and they loved to listen to each other talk. Before the baby, they had been a team. They had gone to the bars, they had talked on the phone almost every night: they were best friends.

But now Louise was in the world of babies, and June was excluded. Louise liked to talk about laundry soap and teething, about rashes and nursing. Now Louise had found other women like her. They were everywhere, apparently, and as soon as you had a baby they found you. They found you in the checkout lanes of grocery stores, in the Laundromat, walking down the street, on a park bench, in the children's section of the library. It was a subcult, a secret club of new mothers, and June was excluded forever; and it was because of Bill, not that she hadn't agreed, but it was his idea.

"June!" Louise called, when she saw her friend. She was sitting at a booth. Louise had thick black eyebrows and blonde hair, bleached, the roots showing now. She wore one of her husband's old white T-shirts, and it was stained in the front with milk. Her breasts were large and pushed against the shirt. She wore a pair of old blue jeans, tight at the waist now, from the fat she hadn't lost yet, but Louise was beautiful, June thought. She was a woman with wide green sleepy eyes and creamy skin, and June suddenly wanted to run her hand over it. Louise was always warm. "June!" she repeated, needlessly. Nobody in the north said her name the way Louise did. Nobody knew how to stretch that *u* sound out.

The baby was lying on the booth beside Louise, asleep. The baby, they always called him, because his name was Charles, and Charles didn't seem right for a baby and neither did Chuck, and Louise didn't want Charlie, although that was one of June's favorite names. She slid into the booth across from Louise.

"He's sleeping," said Louise, but June could see that for herself. "I think he's getting a tooth," she added.

"He's only a month old."

"Six weeks," corrected Louise, adding, "He's fussy."

"He doesn't seem very fussy."

"Well he is."

"Babies don't get teeth yet."

Louise gave her a look that said, *who are you to talk about babies?* "Babies are all different, you know. This baby"—and here she looked down at him—"is in a big hurry to grow up." Addressing the sleeping baby, she whispered, "Aren't you? You are just in a big, *big* hurry."

What if babies are conscious the way we are? June wondered. What if babies are trapped in their little bodies, waving their arms and legs helplessly, unable even to hold their heads up? What if their cries are cries of terror?

Louise looked up suddenly and, misinterpreting her expression, asked sympathetically, "Haven't you ever thought of adopting?"

"Adopting? Adopting a baby, you mean?"

Louise shrugged. "Or an older child. A hard-to-place child. You could adopt Cindy." When June didn't respond, Louise added, "A girl needs a mother."

"Bill doesn't want kids."

"She's pretty old anyway."

"She's only ten."

"Well, then."

"She's not up for adoption."

"Maybe she should be."

"Bill doesn't like kids."

"How can he not like kids? A lot of guys think they don't like kids, but then they get one of their own and they are so glad. Sally Steele, remember her? She was always dying to have babies, but then she married that Petefish boy—Howie Petefish, he didn't want any kids. So there she was, taking care of her nieces and nephews and saying it was almost as good, but it's just not the same, everybody knows that, and then they go and divorce. *He* leaves her. She worshipped the ground he walked on, always did." Louise paused and then added, "She was older than what he was."

"Only five years," said June.

"Still." The baby, Charlie, began to fuss. Louise picked him up and began to pat his back. Her hand was almost as big as he was, and June thought suddenly of Mikey. "And so he leaves her and, guess what, next thing you know he's married to Connie Blowmeir, and they've got a baby." Louise held the baby out and looked at him. "Howie's just nuts about that baby. Just nuts about it." The baby had settled down again, and now she laid him back down on the bench beside her. She always told June the baby took so much time she couldn't even cook dinner anymore or clean the house or wash her hair. That was what new mothers always said, but as far as June could see, babies just slept all the time, and how much work could that be?

"Men don't know what they want," Louise concluded.

Two women were wiping down the tables. Darrel's didn't have waitresses who came to you with a pad of paper. They had girls who took your order and then later when you were gone, cleared and wiped your table. The girls wore white A-line dresses, very unflattering, June noted, with black-and-white checked aprons. They tied their hair back.

"Ma'am," called the girl from the table next to them, "you need to order over there." She addressed Louise, pointing to the counter. "We don't come to your tables, you know."

"We're just deciding," Louise replied, and then she turned around completely in the booth, to face her. "Too bad about that girl who got killed," she said.

The woman stopped what she was doing and came to stand at their booth. She had a name tag, Tami, it said. She had her hair pulled back, and it was greasy. "She used to work here," she told them. "You probably read it in the paper." She waited expectantly, and when they nodded, she said, "Course, I knew her. She was a friend of mine." She looked around, but no supervisor was in sight. The only other people in the restaurant were the girl behind the counter and another woman, a big blonde, who was wiping tables. Tami leaned forward. "I was almost working the night he got her. He got her from here, you know." The girl stopped and looked around again, but this time she wasn't looking for her boss. She was making the point. It started right here. Just imagine!

"He came *in* here?" asked June.

"He didn't get her from here, Tami!" the big blonde corrected her. "He got her walking down the street."

But Tami stuck to her guns. "I seen him in here before."

"He got her walking down the street." The other woman came to their booth as well. She said, "My cousin has a boyfriend, works at the police station, and she told me he said that he heard one of the cops say how Pruett claims he found her walking down the street. He says he is innocent."

"They all say they are innocent," said Tami.

"I'm just telling you what he says."

"He's a killer. You think a killer won't lie?"

"There was the blood in his car," Louise reminded the second woman.

"Pruett said she fell down."

But this was Tami's story, and she interrupted to say again, "He came in here before." She turned to June. "He sat right where you're sitting."

The big blonde rolled her eyes and moved on.

"Had a vanilla malt, a double cheeseburger, and fries, and didn't even leave a tip."

"Did you see him more than once?" asked Louise.

But Tami was suddenly suspicious. "You're not reporters, are you? We're not supposed to talk to reporters."

"Do we look like reporters to you?" Louise raised her eyebrows.

"We just came in to get a milk shake," said June, and to prove it, she stood up and walked to the counter. A girl came out from the back and took her order. June could hear Tami and Louise talking, but when she returned to the booth, they were quiet.

The sound of the milk shake machine was loud, and the baby began to fuss. Louise lifted him up. His head flopped a little, and she steadied it with her hand.

"Those are her shoes," said Louise, nodding to the red shoes. They were out of place, red high-heel shoes that June wore with her blue jeans. "I told her you were Vernay's sister," said Louise to June. "I hope you don't mind."

June didn't see the point to this new lie, but she stretched her legs out, into the aisle, to display the shoes. She turned them to the left and to the right.

Tami looked doubtful. "The papers didn't say nothing about a sister."

"Sister-in-law," June said.

"She got all her clothes," added Louise.

"You lucky duck!" said Tami, and then she leaned forward and said quietly, "Mimi"—she nodded to the skinny girl behind the counter—"took her shift that day. See, she was supposed to be working, but she got Mimi to take her shift, she was always wanting somebody to take her shift, and that day Mimi did it, and then she went and got herself killed."

The women turned to look at Mimi now, and Mimi, misunderstanding, held up their milk shakes.

"I thought you said she was here when he got her," said Louise.

"She was walking down the street!" insisted the big blonde.

"She was supposed to be here," said Tami, frowning.

June got up and went to the counter. She paid and took the milk shakes from the girl named Mimi. Cindy had said that the women who worked with her mother were jealous, and June wondered if this was true. The girl Mimi might have inadvertently saved the life of Vernay, if only she had refused to trade her shift that day. And June watched her, thinking this, wondering if it had occurred to Mimi, or if she was the only one who thought this way.

"You want something else?" the girl asked. "You want fries?"

When she got back to the booth, Tami turned to her. "I thought her brother had a divorce. The papers said he had a divorce."

"Oh, the newspapers!" said Louise, and she made a motion with her hand to wave those newspapers away.

Tami had taken too long with this table. She wasn't even a waitress. She had no reason to spend so much time with the customers. She could lose her job if she wasn't careful. She moved away to finish wiping down the other tables and booths.

Louise leaned across the table and spoke in a loud whisper. "I didn't think we were supposed to tip in places like this. Not when we go to the counter ourselves and put in our own order and everything."

"If someone is in the mood to kill a person," June said, "then how hard do they try?"

"What are you talking about?"

"I'm asking how much effort do they put into it." June leaned her chin into the palm of her hand. "Do they keep at it, or after a while do they get hungry and go home for dinner instead? Maybe they think, Well there's that TV show on, and I hate to miss it."

Louise shrugged. She drank her milk shake. She drank it fast, and whenever she pulled away, June could see lipstick around her straw, in a circle. The door had a buzzer attached to it, and every time someone came in or went out, that buzzer sounded, and Louise turned to see who the heck it was, like someone interesting might come through the door of Darrel's Hamburgers. June thought, I don't think so. Well, except for Ralphie's father, and he was only interesting because of this one thing.

"Why do they do it, Louise? What is satisfied, and how can it be worth killing somebody? Does it make them happy? Does it make them happy while they do it, or does it make them happy later too, thinking of it? Does it make them feel special? When they pass you on the street, do they think, ha ha if you only knew?"

"Jeez, June!"

June was quiet. She was morbid, that was what Bill always said. She remembered the conversation with the waitress and asked, "Why did you say I was her sister? What was the point of that?"

"Sister-in-law," said Louise, but that made her think of Harlan. "What's he like anyway?"

"Harlan? He's okay."

"The teacher said incest, didn't she?"

"It wasn't a teacher."

Louise leaned forward and whispered, "Incest!" like the word alone was enough to convey the urgency of the situation.

"It was more of a rumor, I think."

"You know they keep files on the kids. It seems like there'd be some way—"

"No!" June said, but she said it too loud, and Louise

looked down at the baby. Charlie. His name was Charlie, and June was going to start calling him by that name. It was a good name, a friendly, dependable name.

"Incest in the family—that's what was said."

"Someone said that, but it doesn't mean it's true. And it doesn't mean it's the uncle." June looked away. She wished she could have a cigarette in Darrel's Hamburgers, but there was a law that nobody could smoke inside businesses anymore, even if they were restaurants, and anyway Louise wouldn't let her smoke around Charlie. Louise was never careful before, but this is what children do to you, June thought.

"You think he's a weirdo?"

"I said I think he's okay."

"But you can't tell, can you? That's the problem. You can't tell about people."

"You mean people can't tell about people, or I can't?"

"Sometimes you're too trusting, June."

"I don't know why you say that!"

Louise lifted her eyebrows. "I'm just saying that sometimes you're too trusting."

But this didn't clarify anything, and June frowned. "*I'm* just saying that sometimes you get a feeling about a person."

"Like you got a feeling about Pruett?"

"Do you want to argue with me? All I can say is what I know, and all I know is he seems nice enough to me."

Chapter 8

O n Thursday her car wouldn't start. She had left
work late, and now she sat in the parking lot while
the bell rang, and the parents picked up their children, or
children walked or climbed on the school bus, and her
engine wouldn't turn over. She looked at her watch.

Bill would have left for work by now. Dinner was hours
away, and Bill was the chef, which meant someone else did
the prep for him. Someone else chopped the vegetables,
steamed the potatoes, made the salad dressing. She sat in
her car. She thought of how many invisible things people
did for us, things no one thought twice about, things no one
noticed or remarked on, things we took for granted. She
popped the hood. She wished she could take her car for
granted.

She got out and was looking at the engine when Harlan
pulled his truck up behind her car.

"It won't turn over," June called as he walked toward
her, but Harlan wasn't the kind of man to take someone's

word for it. He had to try the ignition himself, like there might be some special way of turning the key that she didn't know about.

If it wasn't for this car, she thought, she would never have met up with Ralphie's father that day, and this whole thing wouldn't have started. Cindy Hanks would be just one more kid at school she felt sorry for, that's all. But now everything was different. Now, because of a car, everything had changed.

Harlan looked under the hood, but June was not going to stand next to him pretending to be interested. She didn't care about electricity, but she used it. She didn't care about plumbing. There were many things she used and didn't understand. She leaned against the car with her arms crossed in front of her.

"You need a new starter switch," said Harlan.

She said, "I don't have time for this," like it was his fault.

"I can get it for you today."

She remembered that he worked for the salvage yard down the road.

"I could have it done by tomorrow."

"No," she said. "Thank you."

"I got a tow bar at home."

"I don't need it towed." He was a guy who didn't take no for an answer. "Look, I've got towing on my insurance, so I might as well use it. I just had it repaired—"

"But I can fix it."

It occurred to her suddenly that she had never mentioned her husband, and she thought now maybe she should work it into the conversation. *My husband can do it.* That was what she was supposed to say now. *Thank you, but my husband will take care of it.* That would put the right perspective on everything. But her husband wouldn't take care of it, not really. He didn't like to work on cars and, anyway, he was always gone. When would he find time to do it? He stayed out until all hours of the night sometimes. Some days he went to work three hours early.

"Look, I said no, okay?" Maybe not mentioning her husband was a lie, or like a lie, she didn't know. She had never been one to hide things from people before, and she saw how it could become a habit.

Harlan frowned and looked down at the pavement. He said, "Anyway, I'll give you a ride home. Surely you'll let me do that."

She rode beside him in the car. She was not going to mention her husband, she could see that now. She rode, looking out the window. If Bill found out she'd taken this ride, he wouldn't like it. He was jealous, but he wouldn't say that. He'd say, *June, you can't be too careful.* He'd say, *There are a lot of nuts out there.*

Had people always said that about each other, *a lot of nuts out there*? And was it the truth or not?

"Where's Cindy?" she asked at last.

"She walked home with friends."

"She's a big help in the kitchen."

But Harlan wasn't thinking of Cindy. He said, "You know that car at my house? All it needs is a new master cylinder, it's Vernay's car, I'm going to get it fixed, and you can just have it. It's an eighty-five, but it's got some life left in it."

She didn't answer him.

"I was going to fix it, see. I told her I would, and I was going to, but you know how things are, I just hadn't got to it yet. I was busy, you know. And the thing is, if she had the car, if I had fixed it like what I said, then she would have driven home that day, instead of taking a ride." He had never talked about the murder to her before. "You don't take rides from strangers, anybody knows that, right?"

"Right," she said.

"The only thing wrong with it is the master cylinder. I wouldn't let her drive it anymore because the master cylinder, it's part of the brakes. I said, you can't drive around with bad brakes. They'd gone spongy, you know. I said to her, 'Vernay, this is something you want to get fixed.' Doesn't that beat everything? It's not safe, I told her."

June wished she could say something to show him it was her own fault as much as it was his, but she couldn't tell him this, and anyway, she was distracted, worrying that someone might see her with Harlan and mention it to Bill. Bill might find out about her visits, which suddenly seemed crazy. Bill said she was obsessive, and he was right. She had lied to Harlan and to the girl. She had taken Vernay's clothes, her shoes, her bra. She had sat in Vernay's room, on her bed. She looked out the window of the car. She said, "You can't blame yourself."

"I brought her here when she was in high school to get

her away from Mom and that mess up in Portland. When she got older, she went back with Cindy—not to Mom's but back to Portland. I always worried about her up there. When she and Cindy moved back here again, I was so relieved. And now look what's happened."

"There's nothing you could have done," said June.

"I would have given her a ride," he said.

"We don't know why things happen."

"I can fix anything wrong on a car."

June wouldn't go back to the Hankses' house again, she told herself. Harlan wouldn't do anything to harm his niece. He was a nice man, a kind man, a man who had a conscience. She would see Cindy at school, but she would step back and let them live their lives the way they were supposed to. She couldn't control any of it, and it wasn't her place to try. She couldn't take back what had already happened. She was married to Bill, and he loved her. He phoned from work and called her *baby*. He could hardly wait to get off work, and she could hardly wait, either. She'd be up when he got home. Other people got tired of each other, but they were lucky. They were special. He leaned against the table next to the flowers and the reservation book and whispered to her. He couldn't get enough of her. That's what he said.

Harlan ran his hand through his hair. "I always looked after my sister," he said. "She's my baby sister. It was just the two of us, and I took care of her. I tried to. Now it's just me and Cindy. People wanted to know why I didn't call the police sooner. The police kept asking me about that. They had their eye on this guy, this nut, this Pruett bastard, they had their eye on him. He beat up a woman in that sports bar on Polk Street—didja read about it? What makes a man like that, I want to know. Back in the old days, I'll tell you what, a girl's father and her brothers, they'd string him up. They'd nail him to a tree. They'd set him on fire."

June turned in alarm to the man beside her, but he looked just the same as usual.

"Back then a man would think twice before he'd hurt a woman." They drove on in silence, and then, after a while, Harlan said, "There's no reason in the world for you to spend money to fix that car of yours. I'm telling you, I can do it for nothing. After what you've done for Cindy, I'd be glad for the chance to give something back."

June pointed to the turn. They were only half a block from her house, and she wondered if it was a mistake to let Harlan know where she lived, but she soon forgot that concern because he said, "Oh, yeah. I know this place. I brought my sister here before; it's that house—the white one. I brought her to see you a couple times."

June swung her head around to look at him. "You brought her here?"

"A couple times. See, I'd give her a ride whenever she asked."

Harlan pulled over and stopped in front of her house, but June didn't think of the neighbors seeing her with a man. She didn't worry that someone might mention it. She wasn't thinking of anything. She was hearing Harlan's words again: *I brought my sister here before . . . I brought her to see you a couple times.*

"When?" she asked, looking at him.

"If you change your mind about the car—"

"When did you bring her here?"

He put the car in gear, ready to go. "A couple weeks ago." He shrugged. "And a few months ago, around Christmas I guess. Don't forget what I said about your car."

He was done with her.

June opened the car door. He had made a mistake, that's all. She got out of the car and shut the door.

He had known the house. *The white one,* he'd said.

Chapter 9

J une went inside and shut the door. She leaned against it
and closed her eyes. It was a red door, lucky. She leaned
against her lucky red door and tried to think of the reasons
why Harlan Hanks might bring his sister here to her house.
The only explanation was that it was a mistake, him making small talk, proving that see he did give his sister rides.
· He had given her rides here to the white house and he knew
it was the white house because June had looked at it or
given some kind of clue.

This is what happens when we begin a tangled web,
June told herself. Because we deserve doubt, we begin to
doubt others. Everything probably begins in an innocent
way. Everything has a beginning, a mountain has a beginning, thunder has a beginning, a lie has a beginning, a murder has a beginning. They all have a beginning, when they
are just small. When something is small, you can stop it, she
told herself. When it is just beginning, you can pluck it out.

Not telling Bill about her visit to the Hankses' house,

that was the beginning of this problem, which was a problem of doubt. Or that was the problem now. She leaned against the door with her eyes shut. She doubted her husband. She had never for a second doubted him, and now she could see how extraordinary that was, to have perfect trust, not a moment of wondering, no hesitation, no guile, nothing but absolute, complete trust.

Everything had a beginning, even murder, and every one of those beginnings must start out seeming logical and innocent, or anyway, not too bad, certainly not unthinkable.

June was not going to sit around all night, waiting for Bill to get back. She was *not* going to wait on the couch, sit on the back steps, wander around the house, call Louise on the phone for her theory. She was not going to make up stories to explain what Vernay Hanks was doing at her house or why Vernay's brother had lied about it, or had he been mistaken? And what was the connection between her and Vernay? She was not going to think about it.

June went upstairs to her room. She took her clothes off and put them away. She looked at herself in the mirror, and she thought how vulnerable people are with their soft bodies, furless, without claws or fangs, without feathers or scales. We are nothing like other animals, she thought. She showered and dressed. She didn't wear Vernay's soft yellow bra. She didn't wear her yellow linen skirt or low-cut white silk blouse. She put on a short black skirt and tights. She wore her favorite lace blouse. She didn't look at herself in the mirror. She looked good, she could feel it, and anyway how she looked was not the point. She put on lipstick, mascara, perfume. She put on a sweater. At the last minute she took off her own shoes and wore Vernay's red high heels instead. She went downstairs and outside.

In the war, museums had been looted and the libraries burnt. A baby's body had been pulled from a building where they said Saddam Hussein, that devil, might have died, but really it was only an elderly couple and a baby. When you hear *an elderly couple and a baby* from way over here, on the other side of the world, you think well that's not so bad, it's a war after all. But what if it was your own baby?

June stood on the sidewalk in front of her house suddenly realizing that her car was across town at school. She had her black pocketbook in her hand. She felt like a woman out of a Tennessee Williams play. It should be hot, she thought. She should be sweating. She looked up and down the street, and then began to walk. The bus stop was half a block away. The last thing June was going to do was sit at home and wait. She passed the Mightymart where everyone went for beer and cigarettes. She went to the bus stop and stood. She had change for the bus in her hand.

She waited by herself. When the bus came, she got on and sat down. It was always a surprise to wait at a bus stop and then have the bus actually come. When she had said that to Bill once, years ago, he had laughed and said that she was someone who doubted everything, but that wasn't true. She was too trusting, if anything. She was gullible. She'd believe anything anybody told her.

June sat on the bus next to a Mexican woman with

shiny black hair and a baby. The baby watched June. He had sad, serious eyes. He sat on his beautiful mother's lap and watched her.

She wondered what it must be like to have a baby of your own, to carry it and feed it and have it lie on your lap, to have it love you and trust you and need you. To have everything you say and everything you do matter to someone. To start out fresh and perfect with another person. She could feel the red shoes on her feet, and they felt like her very own shoes.

When the bus reached downtown, June got off and walked. McMurray's wasn't far. It was by the river. It was spring, and all the rhododendrons were starting to bloom. They came in almost every color. She walked along, not hurrying, and told herself to notice the colors, notice the flowers, notice that it's spring and the day is beautiful. It might rain later, but right now the sky was clear.

June opened the door to the restaurant and was seated. She didn't usually come here, but they all knew who she was. Bill had just arrived, she was told. The host seated her at a small table close to the kitchen. It was Thursday, and the dinner rush hadn't started yet. Every Thursday Bill left home early to go to work, but he had just gotten here. Every Thursday. It was part of his schedule. June asked for coffee. There were empty tables, and the waitress didn't mind the chef's wife taking up a whole table for a cup of coffee.

McMurray's was a nice restaurant. It had clean hardwood floors and a stone fireplace. The tables were wooden, and each one had a bouquet of flowers on it, tulips and daffodils. Purple, red, and yellow. People drove down from Salem. They drove up from Eugene and over from Albany to eat here, but it was too early for them today.

Bill came to the table with a piece of pecan pie for her. He never told her to watch her weight, like other men told their wives. He never worried that she'd get fat. He loved to watch her eat. He loved to feed her and watch her chew and swallow. He liked to put his fingers in her mouth. He liked to touch her lips.

He sat across from her.

He pushed the pie toward her, but she didn't look at it. He had on his tall white chef's hat and a white apron.

June wished it was like any other day and she could take a bite of the pecan pie, her favorite, and he would watch her. She wished they could go home and go to bed and not say a word.

"What's up?" he said.

She was going to start with the day she had gone to Harlan's house and squatted down next to his car and said she was the friend of his dead sister. She was going to walk Bill through the events that led up to now. She was going to ask why he went to work so early some days, but instead she told him about the car. She asked where they should have it towed. She told him a funny story about one of the kids at school. Bill liked stories. He liked people, and he liked food and drinking and pleasure. He liked sex. He was a handsome, sensuous man, and women liked him. He could have had anyone he wanted, and he wanted her. He liked books and music and nature. She could have had anyone too. She could have had Sean Callahan, who was rich, with an airplane and a band, but she wanted Bill. They were the perfect couple, everyone said. They were lucky. They liked each other. They were best friends. And Bill was very funny, and Bill cared about the same things she cared about. He hated the thought of cluster bombs.

She had always been honest with Bill, but now she heard herself talking about the car. She wondered where they should tell the tow-truck driver to take the car. Should they use the same guy they used last time or not? She heard there was a Jehovah's Witness out on Highway 99 who was very dependable. He wasn't expensive either. It surprised her the way she could carry on a conversation about a car just then. And while he talked to her, while he talked about the car and one mechanic versus another, she sat quietly, not eating, her breath shallow, watching him. She didn't know what she suspected.

The restaurant was beginning to fill up, and he'd need to go back to the kitchen, and she would need to give the table up to customers who had come for dinner. The sous chef had already peeked out of the kitchen once, to see where the hell Bill had gone.

"The scallops are really good tonight," he said.

He turned his head toward the kitchen and then faced her again, indicating the pecan pie with his hand. "You've already gotten dessert out of the way. Might as well stay."

He was crazy about her, she knew it. She would go home and forget all about this. Surely she had tipped her head toward their house, and Harlan had read the gesture, and that was all. He had seen her look at it.

Chapter 10

There was an emergency meeting in the library because Mikey had brought a hunting knife to school. The next day the newspapers would be here, and the staff had to be told not to talk to the press. The staff sat at tables, eating chocolates, while Mrs. Dodd, the principal, talked. She said that, according to the psychiatrist, Mikey was the kind of boy who might show up years later and shoot his teacher. They all swung their heads to look at Mikey's classroom teacher, Mrs. Rose.

Mrs. Rose, June knew, could be counted on not to comment. She used to comment, but she had been pulled aside the year before and told to keep her mouth shut at staff meetings. According to Mrs. Dodd, she was a troublemaker, and if she had any comments, she could make them in the privacy of the principal's office. Mrs. Dodd had enough problems. They were a team and a team has to work together, she had told Mrs. Rose. It was a private conversation, but it had been told and retold in angry whispers in the hallway and staff room, even making its way down to June's kitchen. They all looked at Mrs. Rose, and she shrugged. She had two young children and a husband with no job.

June wondered what Mrs. Dodd meant by *the kind of boy*. She knew that people said Mikey had begun to hear voices, but what did that mean? What was the line between hearing voices and her own unwelcome thoughts? And certainly, she told herself, the psychiatrist had this point about killing his teacher all wrong. The students loved Mrs. Rose. She had long hair, for one thing, and the children loved long hair, and she never shouted or lost her temper. She went to all their sporting events and sometimes, on Fridays, she brought her dog to school.

If Mikey were an animal, June thought, he'd be a border collie. Too smart for his own good, but eager to please. Give him a job to do, and he was happy.

The principal said that as soon as a bed opened up, Mikey had a placement in Portland, which meant he was going to the psych ward. Mrs. Dodd kept calling it *Portland,* which was the name of an entire city and painted no picture at all. There weren't enough beds, Mrs. Dodd said. Not enough beds? Go buy one, thought June. And how does a bed open up? She wanted to ask, but surely this was off the point.

Now Mikey would be expensive, she thought.

Sometimes when she looked at the parents, she wondered how they made it, and then she had to remind herself that sometimes they didn't. Sometimes they didn't make it at all.

The staff sat in a circle. They were nice people. They

were people who loved children. They were people who wanted to make things better, but they were not brave. They were cowed by Mrs. Dodd who was nothing but a bully, a PR flack, a phony. She always felt false in these meetings. She told herself, They don't pay me enough to be a phony. Maybe they pay Mrs. Dodd enough, but not me.

The reporters would be outside the school in the morning. Some of the families might want to pull their kids out and send them to other schools. Every student lost was money down the drain. The staff needed to know what to tell parents, what to say to the other children, what to say to people in the grocery store. June made a list in her notebook. She didn't see why she had to come to these meetings. She wanted to know what Mikey had said about the hunting knife. Why had he brought it? Why? She wrote in her notebook.

Mrs. Dodd told them they needed to talk about trust. Trust, said Mrs. Dodd again.

"It takes courage to talk honestly," she said, and one of the new teachers said, "Courage, that's a good word." Some of the new staff members nodded their heads. Now we are being honest, they thought, getting real.

The administrators always talked about trust, about being honest, speaking up. Why didn't people speak up? they wanted to know. They always asked that question.

I beg your pardon, June wanted to say, let's talk about Mrs. Rose. Let's talk about power relations. But she didn't. She had a yellow notebook, even though she was the cook and not expected to take notes. Trust, she wrote.

"There's a lot of angst in this building," said Mrs. Dodd, and she seemed to look at her. June was not good at concealing her feelings, and she tried now to make her face look blank. Enthusiasm was out of the question, but she could aspire to neutrality, she thought. "There's resentment." Mrs. Dodd paused to let that sink in, and then she asked, "Do you know what resentment is? It's a hot burning coal and I'm telling you, drop it. Drop that hot burning coal."

June was certain Mrs. Dodd was looking right at her when she said it, and she turned away from her, toward the hall, and her heart gave a leap for there stood Harlan Hanks, right outside the library door. *Shit!* This was against all convention. Parents were never to listen in on staff meetings, but he didn't seem to be listening in. He appeared to be waiting, and when he saw June looking, he motioned with his hand. June turned around to see if there was someone else he was motioning toward, but there was no one else, and Mrs. Dodd said, "Mrs. Duvall, if you have business to attend to, don't let us stop you."

She looked back at Harlan. He didn't seem like one of the dads, but he wasn't like other men from this town either, engineers or professors, men with flat bellies and no gusto. He looked like somebody who had lived a little. He was a handsome man, but his clothes were dirty, and he needed a decent haircut. If he was an animal what would he be? June asked herself, but she didn't know the answer to that. She gathered her things and stood up to join him.

He had been leaning against the wall, but now he stood up straight, waiting for her, while everyone watched. From a distance, you might think this was her husband or a boyfriend, waiting, but it was only Harlan Hanks, Cindy's uncle.

"I didn't mean to interrupt," he said, "but I needed to talk to you today."

June could feel everyone's eyes on her. "What are you doing here?" she whispered, and she walked down the hallway with him following. She walked toward the doors. She wasn't going back to the meeting.

"Forget it." He made a cutting motion with his hand. "Just forget it. I knew I shouldn't have come."

"Well, you're here, aren't you?"

He began walking ahead of her.

"What do you want?" she asked. She was behind him now, looking at his back.

"Nothing!" He walked through the double doors out onto the playground, with her following. The playground had a map of the United States drawn on the pavement, and they walked over it. A little further on, there was a stenciled message that said, "Safe, responsible, and respectful."

"Hey!" She caught up with him and held his arm. Maybe he'd be a rooster, she thought.

He said, "Look, if you don't want to be seen talking to me—"

It was true she didn't want to be seen with him, but it wasn't for the reason he thought, because he was a rough guy, a poor guy with cheap clothes and a bad haircut. It was because of Bill.

"I was at a fucking meeting," she said, and the fact that

she would say *fuck* in front of him created a sudden, unan-
ticipated feeling of intimacy.

"I guess you got your car running," he said. When she
didn't answer, he added, "I hope you didn't pay too much."

But she wasn't in the mood for small talk.

"You told me that if we ever needed a favor, I should
ask. You remember that. Well, it's for Cindy. Course. I
thought maybe, being's you offered, you could come for
dinner tomorrow night—" He saw the look of doubt on her
face and hurried on, "Tomorrow is Vernay's birthday—she
would have been thirty years old—and I thought we should
have a little dinner, nothing fancy." And then he added,
"They say the first year's the hardest."

On Saturday night while Bill was at work, June got dressed
up and went to the Hankses' house for dinner. She wore
her favorite skirt and her red blouse. She brought a bouquet
of sweet peas. She brought ice cream and root beer.

She had been thinking about what Louise had said about
adoption. Sometimes people held out for the perfect thing,
and so they wound up with nothing. The perfect thing for
June would be her own baby, someone who looked a little
like Bill and a little like her, someone whose only childhood
would be the one she gave it. If she had a baby, she thought,
she'd do everything perfect, from the first day.

She had told Bill she didn't care if they had children or
not. She had meant it, but either she had changed or she
had said it without full knowledge of her own mind.

She wanted a baby, but now Cindy had come along. The more she thought about it, the more it made sense. Cindy wouldn't be the same as a baby, but there were advantages to an older child. They could join 4-H or Girl Scouts. They could cook together and ride bicycles. There were so many mother-daughter activities, now that she thought of it. A girl needed a mother, there was no getting around it, and something, fate if you believed in that, had thrown them together. Bill would like Cindy, if he would just give her a chance. He'd be a good father. He always said he wouldn't be, but that was only because he was too conscientious.

She would explain to Bill everything that had happened with the Hankses, but the story had a different theme, one that would overshadow everything else, and that was Cindy. She had never expected the relationship with the Hankses to last as long as it had, she would tell him. She was sorry about the mother, that was what started it all. She was so sorry about Vernay, whose thirtieth birthday was today.

She knew she wasn't to blame for Vernay's death, but she was involved. There was no getting around it. If she had taken the ride that day, he would have killed her instead and Vernay would be carrying on her life, turning thirty, being Cindy's mother.

Vernay never wanted to be thirty anyway, Harlan had said, as he walked her through the parking lot to her car, but that was just something people said, and they didn't mean it.

She thought of the woman who wanted to be a deer.

The woman with the yellow linen skirt. The woman who liked red high heels.

June had begun to wear her clothes. Nothing obvious, like the shoes, usually, but sometimes the bra, sometimes the white slip, and sometimes she would carry the blue scarf in her pocket. People thought relationships end when someone dies, but it wasn't true. She was having a relationship with Vernay Hanks. She could feel the presence of the other woman around her the same as she had felt the presence of her Guardian Angel when she was a girl. When her father had died, he had disappeared off the face of the earth, but she could feel Vernay looking over her shoulder. She could sense her. Vernay was close by, listening and watching. June didn't believe in ghosts, but she believed in this.

She drove to the Hankses' house and parked out front. She was going to talk to Bill that night. She'd wait up for him and tell him everything. It was just silly not to. If he thought she had gone off the deep end, then that was better than being a liar. She turned the rearview mirror and looked at herself. She put lipstick on and smoothed it with her fingertip. She had read one time that children lie to prove that they have private lives, separate from others, but June had doubts about that theory. Sometimes people lie out of laziness, she thought. Sometimes a lie is an accident; sometimes it's a kindness.

She had put her hair in a French braid, and she had worn her black tights and her brown boots. She got out of the car and walked up the sidewalk toward the house. Vernay's car had been moved to the curb, and now an old red Dodge truck was in its place, up on blocks in the driveway. The grass needed cutting. The yard was full of dandelions. There were some planters out front where someone must have had flowers once, but now they were empty.

She walked up the stairs and stood on the front porch. She was too dressed up. She wondered if she should have come, but already she could hear Little Babe inside, barking, and soon someone would be at the door. She didn't knock. She turned and looked at the old plastic Santa lying on its side in the yard across the street. She looked at the flag.

She brushed her skirt down with her hands and thought of Bill. She thought how she'd tell Bill all these details. He loved the way she made things into stories. He loved the way she remembered dialogue and the way she noticed little things that other people missed. She'd wait up for him. If it were warmer she'd sit on the front porch and drink a beer, and when he came she'd watch him get out of his car. She'd watch him walk toward her. She loved the way he walked. She loved the way his face was when he noticed her. She turned back toward the door just as it opened up.

"I thought I heard somebody." It was Harlan. He stood on the other side of the screen door looking at her. He ran his hands through his hair.

"Aren't you going to ask me in?" she said. She shouldn't have come, and now she was stuck. She was here for the evening, and she had the wrong clothes on, and it was too hot for the tights.

"Sorry." He swung the door open, and she walked

inside. She made him nervous now. He didn't know what to say or what to do with her.

"Something smells good," she said. She handed him the bag with the ice cream and root beer.

He wore a pair of old blue jeans with the knees out and a dirty white T-shirt. He gestured toward her. "You look great. Thanks for, you know, for coming. I know it's a Saturday night, and you got better things to do."

Cindy came in and said hello to June. She wore an apron, and she had tied her hair back. "You can't come in the kitchen," she said. She made a stop sign out of her hand. "It's a surprise!"

June sat on the couch. Harlan hadn't thought to take the flowers, and now she set the bouquet on the coffee table in front of her. She wanted a cigarette, but she didn't want to smoke in front of Cindy. Harlan made her nervous. She couldn't remember him making her nervous before. She was relieved when he went to clean up, he called it, and left her alone. He didn't think to get her a drink or a magazine or to turn a light or the stereo on. She sat on the couch in the quiet and made herself calm down.

There is a place inside each of us that is calm and quiet, she told herself, and she looked for that place. She made herself breathe slowly even though she had never understood the point of that. A cigarette would be better, she thought, but she couldn't have a cigarette. She looked around the room. She thought if she were Vernay, she'd recognize everything in this room. It was getting dark, but she could see things.

The TV sat across from the couch, but it was off. There was a coffee table with an empty package of cigarettes and she picked it up and squeezed it. On the table she saw a box of matches; rolling papers; an old newspaper; a small Phillips screwdriver; a shiny, pink conch shell that was being used as an ashtray; and a pair of toenail clippers. There was a red ball on the floor that must belong to Little Babe, June thought. Little Babe was just a fat old Chihuahua, and Vernay had been a strong young woman, but she was dead and Little Babe was still alive and had a red ball to play with.

June could hear a shower running. On the other side of a wall, Harlan's clothes lay on the floor, and he was naked. Her legs were hot, and she moved them a little apart. She lifted the braid up off her neck. Were the feelings that drove men like Ronald Pruett similar to her own feelings of desire and passion? She couldn't believe it. Anyway, we can't help our feelings, she told herself, but we can control what we say and what we do. Some people don't bother to, but if they wanted, they could. She would never hurt anybody, no matter what her feelings were. She loved her husband. He was a good husband, and he would make a good father. If they had a child like Cindy, they'd be a real family, and all of them—Bill, June, Cindy, and Harlan—would be friends. They'd spend holidays together. On the Fourth of July they'd go to McMurray's annual picnic and the men would play softball.

She ran her fingertip over her lips, wiping the lipstick off. She wished she were in blue jeans and regular old shoes. She wished she hadn't worn her pretty red blouse.

The couch was cheap and plaid. The coffee table was particleboard. The floor was covered wall to wall with a brown shag carpet. Everything in the room was poorly made. She thought it was funny that a man like Harlan, a man who was good with his hands, who could do things, fix things, who understood how things were put together, who spent his life grappling with physical objects, should be surrounded by so much that was poorly made. It made her feel suddenly protective.

She could hear Cindy in the kitchen. Little Babe wandered through the room and sniffed her but then walked on. June picked up the newspaper, but it was too dark to read. She wondered if it had an article about Vernay. Almost every day there was an article. She had been strangled with electrical cord and tossed into the woods. Sometimes there were stories about the Pruetts. Not only Ronald Pruett, the killer, but stories about his family or his house with a truck outside, up on blocks, just like this one. The paper said there had always been troublemakers coming and going. There was a brother who'd been evicted from his own house. There was a friend, out on parole. There was a ripped-up screen door, and the paper always mentioned the truck out front, up on blocks, like it was something dirty.

June stood up and went to the window to look out. If she had taken the ride she'd be dead, and she felt grateful to be alive, to be standing here in her uncomfortable boots, looking out into the night.

A lot of people are alive because someone else is dead, she told herself. Everyone who is murdered might be alive and someone else murdered instead, for one thing. Every car accident could have been someone else. The only difference between her and those other people was that she knew whose life got traded for hers.

There was a reason for it, some people would say, but reason was a human value placed on the way the universe was organized, wasn't it? She wanted to point that out to someone, but Harlan didn't strike her as a likely candidate for this kind of discussion. She'd talk to Bill. She hadn't talked to him since the murder. They used to talk and talk.

She wondered how her life compared to Vernay's. Vernay had a child, but June had people who loved her too. She had Bill. She had people who depended on her. She meant something to the kids at school anyway. She meant something to Mikey Black, though he was leaving soon. Insurance companies had a way to rate someone's monetary value so when there was an accident they knew how much money to pay out. June wondered if you could devise a rating system for someone's true value and if so, what things you would measure. Some of her hair had come loose from the braid, and she pushed it back from her face.

By the time Harlan joined her, June had calmed down.

When she was a Catholic girl, she used to offer up things for the souls in Purgatory. She'd go to the dentist and offer up her pain. She'd have the flu and offer it up. She'd wake up in the morning and decide to be perfect all day and offer it up. She hadn't thought about that for years, but now, as she followed Harlan into the kitchen where Cindy waited for them, she remembered.

She sat at the table across from Harlan. He had put on black pants and a white shirt. He had combed his hair back from his face, and he had shaved. Cindy teased him. "Where's your necktie, Uncle Harlan?" If she was sad thinking about her mother who was supposed to be turning the big 3-0 today, she didn't show it.

Cindy had set the table with candles and plastic place mats. She served fried chicken, green beans, and mashed potatoes. June said she could hardly believe Cindy had made all this herself.

Cindy drank 7-Up and the adults had beer, in cups. Cindy hadn't dressed up. She wore cutoff blue jeans even though it wasn't summer yet. She had pale, skinny legs. She was barefoot. Her hair had come loose and it hung in her food as she ate. They didn't say a blessing; they ate, and Cindy talked.

She said that the only thing her friend Lural could make was SpaghettiOs. She said when she lived with her mother in Portland, they got free food from the church. Cindy added, "We got doughnuts and Oreo cookies." She told June that when she grew up she was going to be a bartender.

June said, "Cindy, you're such a smart girl. You ought to think of a job that uses your intelligence."

"Well," Cindy said, "maybe I'll be a waitress."

Cindy told June she had a glow-in-the-dark gerbil cage for her gerbil, Marge. She said when it snowed last year she had made a snow gerbil. She said she hoped Marge lived a long time, and Harlan said surely she will live a very long time, and June said that's right.

Cindy said she thought Little Babe should be able to sit at the table, but Uncle Harlan wouldn't agree to it, she told June. She said she heard of a dentist over in Eugene who had his office in a school bus, and she wanted to go there. "I heard of a lady who took her dog. She had a little white French poodle with one of them pom-poms on its tail, and she got to hold it in her lap the whole time she had her cavities fixed."

"We're not going all the way to Eugene for no dentist," said Harlan, and when June looked at him, he winked. She didn't know what he meant by that wink, and she looked away.

That was when she saw the bracelet. Cindy was making a joke, but June didn't hear it. She looked over, and Cindy was reaching across the table for the plate of green beans, her arm in front of June, and there on her wrist was one of June's bracelets. June felt her stomach lurch. It was her bracelet. A silver and rhinestone bracelet that had belonged to Bill's mother, who had given it to June, but here it was, inexplicably, on Cindy's wrist.

Cindy said, "I'll be glad when Mikey B. is gone. He's mean."

She couldn't have stolen it. The kids stole things sometimes, but Cindy couldn't have stolen this. June kept it in her jewelry box, in her bedroom, in her house.

"He's mean to you?" asked Harlan.

"He said if I didn't shut up, he was going to kick me in the b-word. He said, 'If you don't shut up, I'll kick you in the b-word, you a-word.' "

"That little shit," said Harlan.

Cindy turned to June. "Is he really going to Montana to live with his father? That's what he said. He said his father is a cowboy, with a cowboy hat and ponies! But that's stupid, isn't it?"

"Are you all right?" Harlan asked June.

"I'm not scared of him, Mrs. D. He doesn't even know how to hit. I seen him hit Sammy one time, and he did it like this—" Cindy illustrated a limp swiping motion with her hands, and the bracelet jingled.

"Mrs. D.?" asked Harlan, looking from Cindy to June. His hands were on the table and now he moved them to his lap.

"June Duvall," June said.

"We call them all Mister or Missus because Mrs. Dodd says it's respectful. We have to say it."

"Where did you get that pretty bracelet, Cindy?" June asked, and her voice sounded the same as always, although her heart pounded.

"It was my mom's!" Cindy held her wrist up proudly, so June could see.

June took Cindy's wrist, gently, and pulled it close to her, to look. This wasn't the only bracelet of its kind in the world, June reminded herself. She was overwrought. She didn't know what had gotten into her lately. Bill was right. She needed to relax, have some fun. Maybe the bracelet looked the same, but looks can fool you.

June pressed her hands together, to steady them. She kept her bracelet in her jewelry box in the bedroom, and there was no way Cindy could have gotten it. There was no way, she repeated to herself.

Cindy touched the rhinestones with the tip of her stubby finger. Her fingernails were bitten down and dirty. "Uncle Harlan said they're not real diamonds."

If there was a way, June couldn't imagine it.

"I wanted to bury her with it, but Uncle Harlan said no I should have it. And, anyhow, she didn't get buried—she got burnt up." Cindy looked at June and, misinterpreting the expression on her face, added, "A lot of people do that now."

"Cremation," said Harlan.

"And we can sprinkle the ashes where we want," added Cindy.

June took a drink of beer. In a little while she'd go home. She didn't have to think about it right now. She'd call Louise, and Louise would think of the logical explanation. Right now she was finishing her meal, sitting at the table, making small, appropriate comments. And later, at home, she'd figure it out. Maybe she'd look in the jewelry box and find her bracelet there. She'd feel so silly then.

"Don't you remember it?" Cindy asked.

"What?"

"The bracelet! You must've seen it before." Cindy paused and then added, "Her boyfriend gave it to her."

June shook her head. "No."

"She never took it off."

Suddenly June began to cry.

"June!" She heard Harlan's voice.

She bent her head down and covered her eyes with her hands. Harlan got up and moved toward her, but June motioned him away. If she let herself go, she would begin to wail and sob—and for what? There was nothing wrong. She was jumping to conclusions. Her bracelet was at home, and later, when Bill got off work, she'd tell him the whole story, and they'd laugh and make it into a big joke. He'd be lying beside her in bed with the streetlamp outside shining through the window onto their skin. It would be like the old days, like it used to be, the two of them, when they didn't need anyone else, and she didn't even mind not having a baby because they were so complete, June and Bill.

"I don't know what's gotten into me," she said.

She excused herself and went to the bathroom. She washed her face in the sink. She wasn't going to start crying again. She hardly ever cried. Some women cried easily, but June didn't.

She looked at her face in the mirror. Her lipstick had come off, but Bill always said she didn't need makeup. She quietly opened the cabinet above the sink. She had removed Vernay's clothes from the house, but she hadn't thought of her makeup. It was all here—lipstick, blush, foundation, mascara. June opened a jar of pink face cream and smelled it. She put it away and closed the cabinet door. Bill didn't like makeup. He liked June the way she was. She had long black eyelashes; she had good skin; her mouth was pink.

"Are you okay in there?" Harlan called, from the other side of the door. Cindy was talking to Harlan, but June heard him send her back to the table.

"I'm fine."

The shower curtain was pulled shut, and Harlan's dirty clothes were in a laundry basket in the corner.

June ran her hand over her hair and then opened the bathroom door.

"You better now?" Harlan asked.

"I'm sorry," June said.

"It was the bracelet, wasn't it?" Harlan said.

But before June could respond, he added sympathetically. "It's always a shock how these little things happen and they remind you of her." He squeezed June's shoulder. "I keep thinking I'll get used to it, but I don't."

Chapter 11

U sually June would help with dishes. She'd clean up after she ate at someone's house. She'd stay and visit. She had good manners. But that night she left as soon as she could. She didn't even stay for the root beer floats, even though Cindy begged her. She walked through the living room to the front door, with Harlan and Cindy following. She saw the bouquet of sweet peas on the coffee table, where she had forgotten them. She went outside and down the front steps, got in her car and drove, but she didn't go home.

It was Saturday night. She drove downtown. She thought of when her Aunt Iva got cancer and how long it had taken Aunt Iva to understand, to take it in, to hear the words, to know what it meant. We protect ourselves, June thought, but she didn't want to protect herself. She wanted to face facts, whatever they were. Vernay had come to her house, more than once. Vernay had gotten ahold of her bracelet, and it was so special she never took it off.

June parked her car downtown and walked along the river to McMurray's. The night had turned cool. Her boots made a loud sound on the sidewalk. It was ten o'clock, Saturday night, and couples were out walking, holding hands. People were going to bars or leaving restaurants. A woman walked a dog.

She went inside McMurray's and was seated. It was closing time, but they didn't mind. She sat at a table near the kitchen. She thought she should go home and wait for Bill, but then sometimes he stayed out late. Sometimes he came home at dawn. They were on different schedules. He liked to go out with the boys after work, but who were these boys, she wondered. She didn't know what she suspected. She was Aunt Iva, taking in a little at a time.

Her waitress was a tall blonde with a beautiful face and beautiful arms and legs and body. June looked around to see if the rest of the staff was beautiful too, but there was only the host, a young Mexican man. A beautiful young Mexican man, June thought, but that wasn't much data to go on. June was having doubts about herself. She didn't seem to notice things. She didn't seem to realize things. She used to think she was intuitive, but she had been wrong about that.

June asked for a glass of pinot. She was the chef's wife; they wouldn't complain if she took up a whole table for a glass of wine. And anyway, it was almost closing time. The host was folding napkins for the next day.

When the waitress set the wine on her table, June asked if it had been a busy night. She asked what kind of dessert they had. What specials had Bill made that evening? "Oh, the salmon with blackberry salsa—my favorite." She sounded nervous to herself, but Nicole didn't seem to notice. Isn't it shocking about that girl they found," June said.

The waitress hesitated. She folded her arms over her chest. She looked at June and then away.

"What a shame," June added.

Now that she understood the purpose of the conversation, the beautiful blonde waitress leaned closer. "We were all shocked!" She looked around, but the only person within earshot was the host, and now she added, "Some of them said she had it coming, but I don't think so. Who has that coming, I say? Who?"

"Nobody," June said quickly.

"See?" the waitress said, like that settled it. "Nobody does. It's just blaming the victim, that's what people do. They don't want to see how it could happen to any of us, so they make her at fault, like you can do something to prevent things like this. You know? It could happen to anybody, is my point." She held up her hands to show she was innocent. "Not that she was any friend of mine, no sir."

June could see the people at the next table, trying to make eye contact with the waitress, but the woman ignored them. "You've got to wonder, if she hadn't gotten fired here, then would she still be alive today?"

When she saw the surprise on June's face, the waitress defended her position, saying, "You know how one little thing affects everything else? One little thing you do. Well, if she was still working here, then maybe she wouldn't have been walking down that same street that day. You never know. That's all I'm saying."

June took a drink of wine. She set the glass down and put her hands in her lap. She twisted her wedding ring and waited. She could feel her body as it pressed against the chair, her skirt and blouse as they lay against her skin. She waited. The people at the next table were ready to pay their bill and leave.

One time June had read an article that claimed that, even though it happens too quickly to observe, people's faces reveal their deepest initial responses. According to the article, if it were possible to watch, frame by frame, we would see liars snarl or grimace before we saw their innocent smiles. But when Bill came around the corner and saw the blonde waitress talking earnestly to her, the expression on his face stayed for more than one frame. It stayed long enough for June to see it. It was alarm. He was alarmed to see the blonde waitress talking to her.

Or maybe this was just part of how weird she had gotten. Maybe it was her, June. She had read about people going crazy and how everything they saw and heard became more evidence of whatever crazy thing they were thinking.

She wanted to ask why he had hidden the fact that he knew Vernay Hanks. What reason could he have? She wanted to see his face when she asked the question because that would be the answer to everything. Even if his face only said it for one frame, she'd see it. She felt a sinking sensation. She felt that her heart had stopped beating for a moment, and she was sinking. Her skin was cold, and she wanted to rub her arms, but she couldn't move, and the man who had known everything about her sat across the table, asking, "Would you like some dessert?" And he motioned to the beautiful waitress. "Give us some pecan pie, Nicole, would you please?"

How he could think about dessert at such a moment, she had no idea, and she held it against him.

"She worked here, didn't she?"

June saw the unguarded moment of panic on Bill's face, or maybe she imagined it.

"She?" he asked, and there was nothing on his face now. Maybe she had asked are the scallops fresh and that's all.

"The girl!" June leaned forward, shooting the words at him. She wasn't going to say that name again. The girl she had felt sorry for. June had sat on her bed, in her little pink room with the ridiculous stuffed cat, and she had felt sorry, but she was finished with that. She watched her husband Bill, this stranger across from her, Bill, and the words of Laura Nyro's song came unbidden into her mind, *I love you so, I always will,* but she ignored them.

They were silent as Nicole set a piece of pecan pie in front of her. As soon as they were alone again, she leaned toward him. "Why didn't you tell me? Why didn't you tell me the dead girl worked here?"

"Oh for Christ's sake, June!" He ran his hands over his face. He said, "What is the point? Yeah, she worked here. So fucking what?" He talked in a low voice. He leaned close and looked into her eyes. "So fucking what?" he said again, like he had found the exact phrase he needed so why say something new?

June leaned back in her seat. She had the fork in her hand, and now she used it to smash down the pie. She smashed it down from one end to the other, flat. She didn't look at him now. She didn't want to see his face anymore. She looked at her pie, all the pecans on top, sugarcoated. "What was the point in pretending—"

But he cut her off. "By the time I realized that the dead girl was someone who had worked here, it was clear that you had gone off the deep end, June, and I didn't want to make it worse." She looked up. He was watching her like she was someone to feel sorry for, but it was a trick, she thought, and she wanted the other Bill back, the one she trusted. She wanted to talk to him about this problem she was having. She needed his opinion. He shrugged. "If you want to hold that against me, be my guest."

She had never been suspicious of Bill before. He was a good husband. He was wild about her. He was everything she wanted. She took a bite of the pie and crossed her legs.

"I don't know what's gotten into you lately," he said, but his voice was kind.

The blonde waitress had begun to sweep the floor, and soon June would have to leave.

"Why did she come to our house?"

She wanted the old Bill, but now there was just this man who looked like an animal when it's cornered, when it can't get out, when it has no place to go. June wished desperately that he would say something to make it all a big joke, that he would reach across the table and take her hands, put her fingertips to his lips, call her *baby*, and it would be just Bill and June, that lucky couple. But he didn't. He scowled at her. He said, "I don't know what you're talking about."

"She came to our house!" June shouted, and then she glanced around the room and saw the waitress and the handsome Mexican host turn to look at them. "She came to our house," she repeated, in a quiet voice this time, but hearing it again and hearing it said calmly didn't make it any less horrible. She pushed her plate to the side of the table and leaned close to Bill. "Her brother told me he took her there more than once."

"Her brother? What the hell were you doing talking to her brother?"

"What was she doing at my house, Bill?"

"For God's sake, June, what's gotten into you?"

"What's gotten into you, Bill? What's gotten into *you*?"

Bill sat quietly across from her. He had on his white chef's apron, but he had taken the hat off. He smoothed the apron over his knees and sighed. The next thing he said would be important, everything maybe. She had caught him, or else there was a logical explanation—but what could that be?

"The woman was losing her job here," he said finally. "She just wasn't cut out for a nice place like this. It was too bad. You know she had a kid and everything. June, what did you think? I gave her some tips, but it was no use. I mean she wound up at Darrel's Hamburgers. That was where she belonged, a place like that. She just didn't belong in a nice place. She couldn't pull it off." He was looking around the restaurant, and now he turned back to June. "She was a nice kid, but she couldn't pull it off."

It was time for her to go. They needed to finish cleaning up, and she needed to leave, but there was something else.

"And the jewelry?"

Bill looked puzzled.

"The bracelet," she added, and she circled her wrist with her fingers.

"I don't know what you're talking about." Bill stood up to tell her it was time to leave, no more delaying, time to go out the door and leave them alone to finish their work, cleaning up, counting the money, getting ready for the next day.

She stood up too, but she wasn't ready to leave. "She had one of my bracelets!" she said, standing close to him.

"I don't know what you think, June, and I don't know what you're talking about, one of your bracelets—"

"From your mother."

He was holding her arm, leading her through the aisle of tables, toward the lobby with its big desk and reservation book, its telephone and vase of flowers, toward the door.

"It was in my jewelry box!"

He opened the door and she went outside. She thought he would push her away now that no one was watching. She thought he would push her away from him and say *Go home!*

Like she was some stray dog that had followed him to work and wouldn't leave. But he didn't. He said, "Oh, June, I don't know what's come over you. I don't know what's wrong. You go home, and I'll be there as soon as I can."

Chapter 12

She had forgotten how to understand what was happening. She had forgotten how to read things, how to read people, how to know what the truth was. She used to know these things. She used to trust her judgment. She was a good judge of character, that was what she had always thought about herself. She was going to be careful now. She was going to pay attention. She was going to learn again how to tell the truth from a lie, to recognize pretense, how to move toward honesty and beauty. She wasn't going to fool herself anymore.

She got in her car and drove home. She thought, Maybe I'll just keep driving. Maybe I'll drive to Portland and get on an airplane, or maybe I'll just drive. In the movies they made driving look like freedom, but June didn't like driving. When she was young she used to hitchhike, but girls didn't hitchhike anymore because they had found out about men like Ralphie Pruett's father. She thought, Men like that, they don't have to do anything to you, all they have to

do is get in the newspaper, and they've had a kind of vic-
tory over you.

She drove home and parked in front of her house. She
thought of Mikey Black and his mother. We are at the
mercy of others, she thought. She thought of Louise's baby,
his back so small it could be covered by a woman's hand.

Other people have been through this, she told herself.
She walked to the front door, and her shoes made a dull
sound on the sidewalk. An affair—it sounded so regular
and common. She unlocked her door and went inside. She
didn't turn on the light. She was usually afraid of the dark,
but now she wasn't.

She went straight to the bedroom and opened her jewelry box. The bracelet was gone. Cindy's bracelet was the
same one, the one her mother-in-law had given her.

June walked back to the living room. She sat down on
the couch, and she didn't move. She thought she should feel
something sharp, but she didn't.

Maybe there was a simple explanation, she told herself.
The girl had come to the house, and he had given her
advice. But the advice that was necessary—how could anyone give that? She was a working-class girl. That was her
problem, and it was not going to be solved by discussion.
Nice restaurants hired middle-class girls because they knew
their manners. They knew where to put the forks. They had
good teeth. If their kids were sick, they could hire a babysitter. If their car broke down, they took a taxi. And they
never confused their verb tenses. If a nice restaurant hired
a girl like Cindy's mother, it was to work in the kitchen.

June found herself walking back and forth. The girl had been here, in these rooms. Bill said it was so they could talk, but why come to the privacy of his own home? Why not go to a coffee shop, with other people at the next booth? June thought, If a husband has an affair, it must be a million times worse to find out that it happened in your own home. A million was a huge number, but not too big for this, she thought.

Maybe it was true that they had sat here and talked about Vernay's performance at work. Maybe that was the only kind of performance at issue here. They had sat in this room, across from each other, and he had told her, "Don't be too familiar with the customers. Fork on the left. Easy on the makeup." But what about the bracelet? June reminded herself. What about that?

But couldn't there be an explanation? What if—while Bill had his back turned—the girl had slipped into their bedroom, opened the jewelry box, and stolen it? Maybe she was a thief. Maybe she had stolen at work. Bill had invited her here to warn her, and she had stolen from him. Maybe she didn't know the difference between a cheap rhinestone bracelet and a diamond one.

June sat back down on the couch, thinking it out. It was the only logical explanation. Cindy's mother had been caught stealing at work, or if she hadn't been caught, they suspected. And then Bill, being the man he was, the good man, had taken her under his wing, had tried to help. And she had stolen from him. Women fell in love with Bill, and it wasn't his fault. *Bill, I love you so, I always will.* They threw themselves at him, but she was the only one for him. Weren't they good together? Weren't they lucky? June and Bill, that lucky couple.

Chapter 13

*I*t was a warm night, and the windows were open. Bill was in a chair with his feet on the bed next to her, and June noticed how pale and thin they were. She saw that he had little purple veins showing on his ankles, now that he was forty. She thought, Now when did Bill's feet get to be like that? He always had the most beautiful hands and feet. While she was having those stupid thoughts, her heart seemed to fill up her whole chest and press against her ribs, and it beat red and fast, but it occurred to her that she must look calm because Bill said, "You knew all along, didn't you?" And he laughed a nervous laugh.

She had been ready for him to tell her that the bracelet must have been stolen. Cindy's mother wasn't even his type. June was his type. Wouldn't he say that? *June, you are my type, my only type. We knew she was a thief. We suspected it, and see, we were right.*

"I don't know what you mean by all along," she said. "All along? All along? All along?"

"It's just that people know these things about each other," Bill said, "when it happens. When you've lived with someone for ten years, then you know."

She waited to hear what it was that she already knew, but he didn't say. He waited for her to say something. She thought suddenly of Mikey Black. She thought of Cindy Hanks, and she wanted to put her hands over their ears and push their heads away.

"It doesn't mean anything about you and me," Bill said.

June leaned forward on the bed. She buttoned the top button of her nightgown. "Did you have sex with her?"

Bill gave her a look to say that she was really offtrack, boy oh boy, had she taken a wrong turn, and for an irrational moment she was relieved, but then he said, "That isn't the point," and she knew he meant yes.

Chapter 14

*I*t had been three days, and in those three days June and
Bill had done the same things they had always done.
Maybe, June thought, something else was required of her.
She had confronted him, and he had confessed. It was her
turn now, but she wasn't taking it. Maybe there was something she was supposed to do, but she didn't do anything
different.

In the mornings, June sat in the kitchen and drank a cup
of coffee. The paper was on the table, and June looked for
articles about Ronald Pruett. Every day a new story
appeared. Sometimes there was a picture of him, and sometimes there was a picture of Cindy's mother. It was spring,
and the azaleas were in bloom. Tiny yellow finches perched
on the pink blossoms of her apple tree. The cat next door
was in heat. June drank her coffee, and she told herself
about the azaleas, the finches, and the cat next door
because she remembered they were the kinds of things she
used to notice. She went to work, and she worked. She

came home, vacuumed, and washed the dirty clothes. She made dinner. She sat at the table, but she didn't eat. She went outside and sat on the porch. She could see the rosebush, but there were no buds on it yet. They would be yellow roses, which meant forgetfulness, and when they bloomed she would fill the house with them. She thought, This is what the shell of a life is like when you take away what's inside it, and all that's left is the outside. She thought there must be a therapeutic name for it.

On the fourth day June went to her doctor, Dr. White. She told him what had happened and asked for sleeping pills because she hadn't slept since the conversation. The whole way to the doctor's office she had cried and pulled her hair, and even when she thought, What about the people in the car next to me looking over? she didn't stop. She thought, This is what happens when you go crazy. One day you're just normal, and then someone says something to you, and after that everything is different. You lay in bed at night with your husband next to you, and you want to stab him.

Are we all just one conversation away from losing our minds? she asked herself.

Dr. White wrote a prescription for sleeping pills. He was only a little older than June, but he was fatherly. She sat in his exam room next to him, and she thought, I bet Dr. White is a good husband. He didn't make her hurry up and leave after he wrote the prescription, he just sat there looking at her kindly. He wore a gold wedding band, like always, but that day he twisted it with his fingers, which might have been a metaphor, but what kind of metaphor? She didn't know.

June knew she looked like a mess. When you're thirty-three, it isn't like when you're twenty. When you're twenty you don't stop looking good just because you've stayed up for three nights. And when you're twenty and you cry, you look sweet and beautiful.

The girl from Darrel's Hamburgers had been almost her age, but June didn't want to think about her right now.

"A lot of marriages have problems," June said to Dr. White. She wanted him to see that she hadn't lost her perspective. "I think about all those people walking around looking normal, but a lot of them have the same problem as me, isn't that right?"

"There's a lot of pain in the world," said Dr. White.

Dr. White's office had a poster of the inside of an ear. It had another poster of the heart. There was a *National Geographic* on the desk for you to look at while you waited, and pamphlets about breast cancer and colon cancer.

June told herself, Some people sit here and find out they are going to get sick, suffer for a long time, and then die, but she couldn't rouse her sympathy for them. Instead she thought of Bill and Cindy's mother working together. She thought of the dead woman in her lacy yellow bra, handing in orders, saying, "Bill, can you make this a rush? Bill, can you heat this up?"

She thought of him saying things back like, "Baby, I can heat it up. I can heat it up for you." Which is how he'd talked to June when they first met, and he was the cook and she was the waitress. And now the woman was dead, so Louise said June should forgive her, but June didn't see why. Now that she was dead, Bill could love her forever. Like President Kennedy: you forget the Bay of Pigs and Vietnam. Now that Cindy's mother was dead, she could be any way Bill wanted. He said he had broken up with her, but June didn't believe him. He said she had come over that last day, and he had made her leave.

The doctor wrote a prescription for sleeping pills, and then he said there was medication to get her through this, which meant an antidepressant. This is what we do now, June thought. We take medication because we are so weak we can't even get through the normal heartbreaks people have always gotten through. But then, who could imagine that regular people you see every day, walking around on the street, could get though something like this? June said, "No, thank you," and she stood up to leave.

"You might consider seeing someone to help you through your feelings," he suggested, and June said she had to get back to work, like she thought he meant right now. She looked at her wrist where a watch would have been, if she'd remembered to wear a watch.

June didn't drive past the restaurant on her way back to work but went straight to school and pulled into the parking lot. It was a sunny day, but the kids were inside. Spring fever, that was what everybody had, and she thought of Bill and the girl. "Hot stuff coming through," he would have said, when she walked by with dinner plates balanced on her arms.

June walked across the parking lot. She walked past the empty playground. She unlocked the door to the kitchen and went in.

She thought, In a school kitchen, there is nothing to worry about. There was just her and the kids. But in a normal restaurant, there are the cooks and the waitresses, the busers, the owner, and the manager. There is the meat man, the fish man, the soda man, and the equipment man, all of them, coming in and out. There is all kinds of activity, all the time. There is INS too. And the customers, of course, who think they are the only show in town. The customers are out front, with their personal dramas, and the staff is in back, with theirs. A restaurant is full of passion. You don't want your husband working in a restaurant because of that. Because of all the food and the smells and people sitting at tables and people running in and out. It's a very unstable place, a restaurant, and having a husband who works in one, well, you might as well have a husband in a rock band.

In Bill's kitchen, it was all those people and him, but in June's kitchen, it was her and the kids and sometimes the Vietnamese custodian, Frank Nguyen. Frank set up the tables every day, and then, sometimes, he came behind the line to help. He had a gold wedding band on his finger. You would never catch Frank Nguyen saying, "Hot stuff coming through."

And if Frank's wife cheated on him—which she would never do in the first place—but *if* she did, Frank would not take medication. *Cheat*, it was a funny word. Like having an ace hidden up your sleeve.

June usually talked to Frank while they worked, but that day she didn't say anything. She hadn't slept for three nights, but she wasn't tired. She had stopped crying, and she wasn't pulling her hair. She was at work. She was getting food out of the refrigerator. She was doing her job.

Bill had said, "You look better when you're not crying."

She couldn't remember much of what they had said, but she remembered that.

Bill said that Vernay was always happy, and that was one of the things he had liked about her, how happy she was. He had broken up with Vernay because of June, he said. Like she should be grateful. The last time he saw Vernay, the very day she had died, they had fought, he said. He seemed to expect commiseration from June, his old friend, but she had only said, "Oh fuck you anyway." Maybe there would come a day to forgive and forget, but June couldn't fathom it.

Bill said that his relationship with Vernay didn't have anything to do with the two of them, but he must have heard that in a movie someplace.

Bill said that when he started seeing Vernay, their marriage had improved, which was another thing he must have heard in a movie. It embarrassed June that he would say such a thing and say it with sincerity, like it would be a point of interest to her, something to weigh into the equation of her husband's betrayal.

Bill said, *Hadn't she noticed?*

She did notice that he collected everything she said now, like he was preparing a case against her.

Bill asked, "Wasn't there ever anyone else for you, in all these years? Wasn't there ever any other man you were attracted to? Wasn't there?"

"Yes," she said. "But I never did anything about it."

"Who?"

"Everyone gets crushes."

"It was Bob Papadopolis, wasn't it?"

"Louise's husband? No!"

"Do I know him? Was it someone at work?"

June was standing at the counter, waiting for the kids. Mikey Black was on one side of her and Missy was on the other. They were serving corn dogs again.

June was just fine. She hadn't eaten for three days, but she wasn't hungry. She felt a soft tap on her arm and turned around to see Frank beside her, handing her an apple. He said it was for cook's day, which was a joke. There was a principal's day and a school secretary's day and a teachers' day, but there was no cook's day, she knew that.

Frank had come from Vietnam as a small child in a boat with his aunt. Most of his family had been killed in the war, but he didn't hold a grudge.

We killed three million of them, June thought, and now our politicians shrugged and called it a mistake, like if someone took a wrong turn driving, like if you added a column of numbers incorrectly. But Frank was not bitter. How could he not be bitter?

"Cook's day," he repeated, smiling at his own small joke.

June began to cry.

"You're crying!" Mikey Black shouted. The kids didn't want you to cry. It went against everything.

She should take Mikey to her car right now, June thought, and the two of them should start driving. They would drive and drive, until they had driven out of the lives they had and away from the people they knew, Bill and Mrs. Black to be specific, finally emerging someplace else with new identities. It seemed to her that somewhere this other life already existed, and they could just drive to it. When they woke up in the morning she'd make him breakfast.

The love you give to a child isn't squandered like the love you give to a husband, she thought. It was a bitter thought, and maybe, it occurred to June, she was becoming a bitter person. Maybe it starts like this.

June could hear the doors open and the line of children begin to file in.

"Go!" said Frank Nguyen. "I'll do this. You just go."

She wasn't sure where he wanted her to go, but she left. She walked through the kitchen and out the back door. She stood outside by the garbage cans, but she didn't smoke. She thrust her hands in her pockets. If I had my purse, I'd walk through the playground, she thought. I'd get in my car and go home. Or I'd walk through the playground, get in my car, and go to the restaurant. If I was one of those women with a gun in my purse, then I'd go shoot Bill, but it so happens that I am not one of those women with a gun. See, she thought, you paint yourself into a corner without even knowing it.

She went back inside and saw that Frank had taken her place at the counter. She got her pocketbook, and she went to her car and drove home. When there is a divorce, people say it's too bad for the children, or they say, in a case like hers, at least there aren't any children—but June thought if there was a child it would be easier.

The Buddha says that life is suffering, but he didn't mean it like it sounds. Louise had explained what it meant and June had understood, but she couldn't think of it now.

She went home and sat on her front porch. I can do anything I want, she told herself. It's like when you get a fatal diagnosis from a doctor, then you can go on a big trip and throw your money away. You can charge everything. You can say what you want to anyone, you can get a boat and stand on the deck naked as it sails to Tahiti, you can do whatever you want. The problem with all this is by the time you get to the point where you can do anything, it's not worth the effort. Anyway, she said to herself, I should file for a divorce. That's one thing you do.

Chapter 15

When she thought of Bill, it was almost like he was her brother, a twin, like someone just meeting them might ask, *Are you twins?* Not that they looked alike. When she thought of Bill, it was almost like thinking of herself. When she thought of him, it was like she could be in his skin, like she could see with his eyes, like she could live in him, like she could look down and it would be his hands at her sides. And now he was her enemy. He slept in her bed. They had sex and it was as good as it had ever been. How could that be true, and was it true for him too? She wondered but did not ask. It was a new period of not asking. She had told him everything before, but he had not told her everything. It was a new period of holding back. It was a new period of suspicion, and she wondered again and again, How can it be worth it? People have affairs, and how could an affair be worth it, when it took away everything? June wasn't sure how to proceed. She suspected she was doing it wrong. Did a woman in her situation still have sex with her husband? What was the precedent?

She was bogged down in thought.

Louise took her to a yoga class. Before the baby, they would have gotten drunk. They would have gone to Squirrel's and sat at the bar. They would have smoked cigarettes and drank whisky, and June would have said, *That Bill, he's a son of a bitch.* And Louise would have said, *He is.* Louise would have said, *He doesn't know how lucky he was, asshole. He'll be sorry later.* And June would have said, *But it'll be too late then, son of a bitch.* June would have told the whole story, even the parts that embarrassed her. She would have told how he had said, "You knew all along, didn't you?" like she was complicit. *He's a real motherfucker,* Louise would have said, back in the old days. Maybe she would have taken her shoe off and beat it on the bar, Louise's ultimate expression of indignation. Back in the old days, they would have staggered and shouted, and June would have gotten some of it out of her system. Louise would have waved a couple good-looking men over, to buy them drinks and flirt. They would have gone outside to sit in Louise's truck and get high. In the old days they would have done all those things. They would have made outlandish boasts and threats. Maybe they would have used the pay phone outside to call Bill right then and there and give him a piece of their mind.

But now Louise suggested yoga. Things change. That was what Louise told her—easy for Louise to say. Things changed for Louise by getting better.

Louise said she was thinking too much.

They sat on blue mats in the back of the class. The teacher sat in the front of the room in a white shirt and white pants. She had a sheer orange scarf around her neck, and she sat quietly. They sat in *satsong*, which meant silently. June's eyes were shut. She sat in cross-legged position. She was supposed to think of her breath. She was supposed to watch it go in and out, *escort it out*, the teacher said, like she was a guide and was leading her breath along, pointing the way up through her body, along dark passages and out. Breath was very important, the teacher said. But why? Circulation is important too. What about digestion? June wanted to ask. June sat in *satsong* in the back of the class. Instead of quieting her mind and following her breath, she thought of her Aunt Leeann who was divorced.

It was the first divorce June knew. A Catholic, Aunt Leeann would have to go to hell for it, and how could anything be worth that, June had wondered as a child. One question that no longer troubled her anyway.

Aunt Leeann had come to live at June's childhood house with June's older brother and parents and with her own children, twins, and then, shortly afterward, the new baby. For the prospect of later burning in hell, Aunt Leeann had traded her married life for a small room in June's house, shared with her children, and a job, after the baby was born, waiting tables at a bowling alley. Aunt Leeann had flaming red hair, and she wore her bangs straight across her forehead. She smoked and chewed gum, and she licked her lips obsessively. The soles of her feet were calloused and yellow. Aunt Leeann spanked with a switch, but first you had to cut it yourself from a tree in the backyard.

These were the kinds of useless thoughts that filled June's mind when she was supposed to be following her breath, in and out, and that was all, period. She opened her eyes and watched the back of the woman in front of her, a tall woman with a perfect back and spine, like a row of pearls dangling from a string.

June used to look at people and assume she could tell things about them, but now she thought she might be wrong. She might not know anything about anyone. She might have no intuition at all about people. If she could be wrong about Bill, then she could be wrong about anything.

They were breathing in through the nose and out through the mouth. She would leave him.

Chapter 16

O ne night when June was a little girl, she was playing with the twins at her Aunt Leeann's house when there was a phone call. It was dinnertime, and Aunt Leeann was cooking. The baby was almost due, and Aunt Leeann was big. She walked with a waddle.

The phone rang, and Aunt Leeann answered it. She bent her head forward, listening.

"Just hang up!" June's mother said. "Hang up!" She finally took the phone and hung it up herself. The two women spoke in low voices, and Aunt Leeann cried because the phone call had been another woman, saying she was Uncle Joe's girlfriend. She had called Aunt Leeann's trailer at dinnertime while the chicken fried on the little stove, and the kids crowded into the trailer, and outside the sun beat down hot on the metal roof.

June thought, Sometimes things happen to us, and they hold a key, but the thing they hold the key for won't come along for years or even decades.

She was only a little girl at the time, but she remembered that day so clearly. It was the day Aunt Leeann saw her future, laid out before her, in an instant. June wasn't sure if she had seen her own future yet, but she guessed she had. She had seen it when Harlan nodded to her house, *Oh I know this place.*

It had been a week of living at home with Bill who was someone new; someone she didn't know, but wanted. Someone who slept in her bed. He still made her food and left it in the refrigerator. He made pasta salad with roasted red peppers. He made French bread and grilled salmon, cold cucumber soup and panini. He did the same things he had always done, but sometimes now he stayed out even later, and one night he didn't come home at all. June had lain on her side of the bed, on the very edge, all night, not sleeping. She thought, At least when your husband is deceiving you, he has to be careful.

It was May, and there were six weeks left to the school year.

She got up at dawn. She looked at Bill sleeping beside her. She leaned over close and sniffed his face, but he smelled just the same as always. She no longer slept naked. She slept in underwear and a T-shirt. She went to the living room and pulled open the curtain. It was a white, sheer curtain. She pulled it open and sat on the couch, looking out. Years ago, she had planted roses in front of the window, but it was too early for them to bloom.

When it was time, she got dressed and went to work. She hadn't eaten, but she wasn't hungry. The kids straggled in for breakfast. At lunch, the classes came in in alphabetical order, but for breakfast they came as they arrived. June served them sticky buns, or they could have cereal. They could have Cocoa Puffs with chocolate milk poured on it. They carried their plastic trays and talked in loud voices. They pushed.

There was a new boy, Raymond. He came from Salem and he said that over there they had real wrestling, like on TV. He said he had seen The Bruiser at least five times. Missy said that The Bruiser was her mother's cousin's boyfriend, but Ronnijo Stabenow said The Bruiser was her father. Sometimes they'd say things like, "Oh, get out of here, you big fat liar," when another child made an outlandish claim, but no one argued with Ronnijo. They looked at her and sighed. She was lucky to have such a father.

"You know, you look like him," said Missy, and Ronnijo blushed and said, "Thank you."

Their own fathers were long gone, or if they stuck around it was only to throw them against walls, hit their mothers, or shoot up what little money there was, June thought bitterly. But that wasn't fair. Didn't their fathers wait by the classroom doors to walk them home? Didn't they work two jobs, some of them, trying to pay bills? Didn't they see that the kids were dressed every morning and had supper at night? Didn't they love their kids, like everybody should?

June thought Cindy would tell the kids that The Bruiser had once kissed her mother's cheek, but she didn't.

"Are you mad at me?" Cindy asked.

June looked at the little girl, in her plastic apron and her plastic gloves.

"No," she said. "How could I ever be mad at you?"

That day June went home, and she went right to Bill's closet. She grabbed his shirts and suit coat, his jacket and pants, and tore them from their hangers. She grabbed at his clothes with her hands, bunched them up and pulled at them. She thought they'd rip, but they didn't. She knew every shirt, every jacket, every piece of clothing he owned. She tore them down, and while she did it, she made gurgling noises in the back of her throat like someone drowning, and she thought, Is this how Mikey feels before he lights a fire? She felt like she was capable of anything, but all she did was tear the clothes from their hangers and fall on them, crying.

After a while, she went to the kitchen and found her purse for a cigarette.

She sat at the kitchen table and smoked. Then she went back to his closet. She gathered his clothes in her arms and carried them outside. She threw them on the sidewalk and went back in the house. She pulled open his dresser drawers and grabbed his socks and underwear, his blue jeans and T-shirts, everything she could carry, and she threw them out too. She went through the house, collecting his shaver and toothbrush, his papers and books, and she threw them out as well. She was not upset, but relieved. She went to the garage and found old tubes and wires, bits of insulation, two old tires, bricks, jars of screws and nails, and his tool-box. She dragged everything out, all of it. She piled it on the sidewalk, next to the curb. She thought how sometimes you see your future in an instant, and she thought, Now it's his turn.

She went back in the house and wandered around. She hauled his dresser outside. She found an old lamp he had planned to fix, the old vacuum cleaner he had insisted they keep, a broken window, and plastic gallon jars of automotive fluid. She put all those things on the curb. A blue Buick drove by, slowed down, and an old man called to her, "Are you having a garage sale?" June said no.

When she was finished, she went back inside and sat at the kitchen table. She could see Bill's pile from where she sat. She noticed it was spilling onto the sidewalk, and she went back out and slid it over so it wasn't blocking the way of people walking by. She was especially concerned about the blind woman who walked past every day swinging her cane. Eventually June went back inside and sat at the table with her eyes shut. She couldn't imagine what it must be like to be blind. A blind person, she thought, is at the mercy of others. She put her head down on the table. I would never do anything to make him feel this bad, she thought.

Chapter 17

One night she went to McMurray's and waited outside, across the street, looking through the big, plate-glass window. Bill worked in the kitchen, but you never knew when he might walk into the dining room to talk to a customer or chase a pretty waitress. She didn't know him anymore. He was like Ralphie's father, a man with a secret life. She paced up and down. Finally, she circled around to the back of the building. The staff came and went through a door that opened into an alleyway. Every night the male staff (the waiters or host or maybe Bill) walked the women to their cars. You couldn't be too careful.

She put her hands in her pockets and waited. She wore her old blue jeans and a T-shirt. She hadn't washed her hair in days, but she had brushed it. She smoked a cigarette.

Finally Bill came out of McMurray's. He came out the back door and into the alley, walking beside the beautiful blonde who had seated her, who had given her pecan pie, and looked into her eyes with nothing but innocence and goodwill. Nicole, who had said that everything, no matter how small, affects everything else. They came out together. *You can't be too careful,* June had told herself. She was in the back doorway of a furniture store, pressed against the wall, one hand shielding the glow of her cigarette. They turned out of the alley toward the parking lot, and she waited, but Bill never came back. She waited and waited. Maybe they each got in their own separate vehicles, June told herself, but then she thought, No, they are both in his van now, where I used to sit beside him.

What do we know about anyone, and what do they know about us?

What did Bill want from a woman? June wondered. What did he need that he couldn't get from her? Was Vernay Hanks the first one, or were there others? How could June not have known? Did she know all along, but hide it from herself? She tried to stick to these abstract thoughts, in order to avoid the more troubling ones: Bill and Nicole together, this moment.

The next day the new boy was helping in the kitchen, and he hadn't stopped talking since he'd walked through the door.

Usually June paid close attention to what the kids said, but she was distracted by her rent. She couldn't pay it. She didn't have the money. Louise had asked what was she thinking, kicking Bill out before she got the rent check, but it hadn't occurred to her. "Maybe it doesn't seem like it matters," Louise said, "but let me tell you, sister, it will matter plenty when you're on the street."

A lot of the families at Washington Elementary couldn't pay their bills. They got evicted from their houses or apartments. They lost everything they owned, even their kids' clothes, toys, and schoolbooks. They moved in with relatives or friends. They lived in a hotel, a car, or, in good weather, a tent. There was a campground not far from the school and often one of the families would live there. Someone was always staying at the homeless shelter, but the kids didn't like to talk about that.

June wasn't like the parents at Washington Elementary. She was having a hard time, a stretch of bad luck, that was all. She had friends she could call on. She had Louise. She had her mother back in Greenville, and a brother in San Antonio. She could sleep at Louise's if she needed to. She could have a big garage sale, sell the car, and get a ticket to Seattle. She could move to Portland today. There were many possibilities. She wasn't going to end up on the street, but she was going to end up without Bill.

The kindergartners had begun to come through the line with their trays. The line ran out the kitchen door and into the gym. The children were small and sweaty. Their faces were red, and they were hungry, but they didn't push for the most part because they were kindergartners, and kindergarten is the honeymoon period. Only Albert pushed. He pushed Veronica, and he said to her, "Quit pushing!" He made a face, sticking out his tongue and squinting his eyes, and he shouted, "Quit making faces!"

"Knock it off, Albert!" said June. You shouldn't delve too deeply into the psychology of the children, June felt. And you should never hesitate to tell them to knock it off; this she firmly believed. Sometimes she heard the staff talking to them, saying *that's not okay*—as if such bland, featureless language could make an impression. Lately, they had begun to say things like *I like the way Rosie is waiting in line. I like the way Manuel is holding his tray.* It was their new way of talking to the children, but there was nothing wrong with being blunt, in June's opinion.

They stood in a row: Cindy, June, and Raymond, serving pizza medallions and chocolate milk.

Everyone was new all the time, she thought. Kids were new, staff was new. They were all new—from the people working at the coffee shop or washing clothes at the Laundromat to the ones standing at the bus stop. Everyone left, but that didn't mean they were doing something better. If you couldn't get something better, the prevailing opinion seemed to be, at least you could get something different.

She felt like a horse standing at the starting gate, waiting to go, but being pulled back. If she were a horse, she'd be stamping her feet.

When she went home there would be nothing in the refrigerator. There would be no salmon, no pasta salad, no linguini, no wine. This is why women pretend they don't know the bad things they know about their husbands, she thought.

She didn't know where he was staying, but she could guess.

She wondered suddenly if Cindy's mother had recognized Ronald Pruett from school. That would have given her a false sense of security. She wondered what the police had asked Cindy when they talked to her, and if Harlan had been present. She wondered if they had gone down to the station and talked in one of those rooms like you see on TV, with two-way mirrors and a table, or if they sat in the Hankses' living room with Little Babe. She turned to Cindy now, wondering if the girl had asked the cop what animal he would be if he could choose anything.

The kindergartners were finished and the first graders were coming through.

Cindy, June, and Raymond stood behind a plastic strip of window, with room enough at the bottom for their hands to reach out, but high enough to prevent their breath from contaminating the food they served. Cindy leaned around June, her head almost touching the plastic window. "Shut up! Just shut up!" she shouted.

It occurred to June that the whole time she had stood there serving up pizza medallions, Raymond, beside her, had been talking.

"Cindy!" June said. No one was allowed to say *shut up* no matter what the degree of provocation. Some of the boys had begun to shove. "Keep moving!" she called.

"You could get expelled," said Raymond to Cindy.

"They don't expel you for saying shut up. They expel you if you hit somebody, and if you don't shut up, I'm gonna hit you—"

"And you'll get expelled!"

"And ask me if I'll care!"

Just then the door from the playground opened, and Bill walked in. June could hardly believe her eyes, but there he was, standing among the first graders, as tall and formidable as a giant. Adults didn't come in here, unless they were staff. They went to the office first and got a badge, and even then they had no reason to come to the lunch line. The children were excited by Bill, a strange man here in this unexpected place, and they began to push each other and fall down. They shouted and spilled their trays, and Sammy Gillespie and Mitch Blakely began to fight.

Bill was looking right at June, and for an instant she thought he had come back to her, but that wasn't right.

"Bill!" Cindy screamed over the noise of the children. Bill's eyes darted from June to Cindy. He was surprised to see her, but Cindy didn't notice. She ran from behind the counter, pushing through the wild throng of first graders toward him. "Bill!" she called him. She threw herself at him, wrapping her arms around his waist and burying her head in his chest, while Bill's eyes met June's. Then Bill looked away from her, and they were strangers.

"Hey!" June shouted. "What do you think you're doing!" The children were suddenly quiet. They all turned to watch her. They were just small children—it was easy to forget that—they were only six years old. In a quiet voice, she told them, "You go have lunch and behave yourselves."

Meanwhile, Cindy had pulled back to look at Bill, and her face was beaming. She was fucking beaming, June thought. Her arms were cold, and she rubbed them.

"Where have you been?" Cindy asked him. "Where did you go? I missed you so much!" And then a thought occurred to her, and Cindy asked, "Do you know what happened? Did you hear?"

And Bill pulled her forward and pressed her head against his chest, saying, "Shhh," and "There, there. Baby, I'm so sorry." Over Cindy's head, he gave June a look and the look said, *Don't you dare say a word,* as if he were the one watching out for Cindy.

"Asshole," June mouthed. She set down her aluminum tray. Her hair was pulled back in a ponytail to keep it out of the food. Beside her, Raymond was quietly eating the cheese off the tops of his pizza medallions. She knew she should stop him, but she didn't. She picked up a rag and began to clean the counter.

Bill used to come to school sometimes to visit her. He'd bring lunch and they would eat in the staff room together. She ate early, 10:30, and it was quiet in the staff room then. He would bring a basket, with cheese and bread and olives. He'd bring smoked salmon, and once he brought flowers. He was her husband, and everyone here knew it. But then he had an affair with one of the moms. *One of the moms.* He had an affair with the mother of her lunchroom helper. He had stopped coming, and now she knew why. He hadn't been here all this year. When was the last time he came? she wondered.

Cindy was leading Bill toward her, pulling and shouting. This was Bill, her uncle Bill, her mother's friend, Bill. She kept saying his name, Bill, Bill, like it was something sweet.

June and Bill stood across from each other in the kitchen, where June worked every day thinking of him, with the daughter of his lover, and they said, "Pleased to meet you."

June thought it was unfair that just when she wanted to look her best, when she wanted to remind Bill what a big mistake he was making—when she wanted to be beautiful—she could barely bring herself to shower. Her hands wanted to go to her hair, but she held them at her sides.

Bill, on the other hand, looked just fine. He was a neat, tidy dresser, pressed his own pants and shirts each morning, ironed his blue jeans on the crease. He was more careful than she was. If she were meeting him now for the first time, she'd be attracted to him. If he called her later and they talked, she'd still like his jokes. She'd be interested in what he said, and she'd fall in love with him, if she had half a chance.

It was almost time for the next round of lunches. The younger kids would be finished eating and the older ones would come in for their pizza medallions.

Would she fall in love with him if he were married? Would she say to herself, I can't help the way I feel? Would she ask, How could something so good be bad? What difference does it make to the wife? The wife has nothing to do with it. Would she convince herself that she deserves this? We only live once. It was meant to be. Look how happy I make him. Aren't we good together, aren't we special? Aren't we different from everyone else? Or maybe, if she was Cindy's dead mother, she wouldn't have needed to rationalize. Maybe just wanting is enough sometimes.

"Bill hates school," said Cindy. She was holding both his hands and leaning back. If he let go, she'd fall flat. "He never would come here. He wouldn't!"

"You better go now," June said to him.

He didn't even like kids in the first place.

"You can't be on school grounds without a visitor pass," said June, turning away from Bill. She said this to adults all the time. "It's not allowed."

"He's my friend!" shouted Cindy. She wanted to show him her classroom. There was a picture she drew, hanging in the hallway. There was her papier-mâché globe. She wanted Bill to see it. She wanted him to meet her teacher.

But June ignored her. "I'm sorry," she said to Bill, "but those are the rules."

"But he's never even seen my classroom—"

June leaned toward him. "I said go!"

Chapter 18

Sometimes, June thought, you don't want to see any-body else. You want to be morose for a while. You want to be alone and give in to your bad feelings; give in, give up, surrender. Maybe if you do that long enough, it gets to be a habit and then, before you know it, you're one of those nuts walking around, and it's all because you gave in.

June had a voice in her head. All day it said things to her, nervous, worried, accusing, fearful, urgent things. Was she thinking thoughts, or was she hearing voices? Stress, Louise called it, but was it possible that such a simple word could describe these complicated feelings?

Years before, Bill would sometimes come to visit her at school. She'd introduce him to the kids, but which kids were they back then? Maygan Wannemaker? Chip Paisley? How many kids had moved through her kitchen? She couldn't remember them all anymore. She used to know every name. She used to know all the names of all the kids in the school—

four hundred names. But lately she had begun to slip. Once she ran into two boys in WinCo and drew a blank.

When she introduced Bill to any of the kids, he would say, "June has told me all about you." He would say it whether it was true or not. A thoughtful lie. "She thinks you're really special." He knew how to talk to people.

Every now and then, over the years, he brought lunch to share with her. She ate early, before anyone else. They sat at the big table in the staff room, eating. He had been into French cooking back then, but lately had gone more Northwestern—salmon with hazelnut crust or blackberry salsa, tuna marinated in olive oil and garlic.

People say one reason it's hard for a child to lose its mother is because a mother knows things about us that no one else knows, and when a mother dies, there is no one left to know them. But isn't it true of a husband or wife too? She wondered how long she would remember private details about Bill. Would she run into him one day years later, and have to search her mind?

"Where'd you find him?" the teachers had asked. "Has he got a brother?"

He was her husband, but he was also the boyfriend of Cindy's mother. He had gone to their house. He had gone to the room where June had sat on the bed, he had gone to the bed and lain down with Cindy's mother who was dead now, and he had destroyed their marriage which had begun ten years ago. There had been all those other days and nights, ten years of them. There had been all those conversations and jokes. There had been sex and nakedness and food and everything; fights, walks, trips, illnesses, and work. All the things people do, ten years of it, he threw it all out when he lay down in that little bed on the floor. What was their marriage that he would give it up, just like that? Was it one thing to her and another thing to him?

The car radio was on, she realized, and she turned it off. It was hot, and she rolled down the window. She was driving okay. She was on the right side of the road, using her turn signals and everything.

If the marriage was a lie to him, then was it a lie? Did she have to lose not only her present and her future, but her past as well? Did she have to go back now and rewrite it with this new understanding, like when you find out what kind of guy Columbus really was, a religious nut, a rapist and murderer, and then you have to rebuild your entire view of American history? Was it like that?

When she turned the corner onto her street, she saw Bill's car, and then she saw him, sitting on the porch, waiting. He had been reading a newspaper, and now he stood up, folded it, and watched her.

She pulled over, stopped her car, and got out. "What do you have to say for yourself?" she shouted. She didn't care if the neighbors heard. When you have children, you need to be civil during a divorce, but they didn't have children. "You son of a bitch!"

His pile was still at the curb. Some of it had fallen over. Cords, a broken hammer, a carton of paper plates, and an old answering machine had spilled onto the sidewalk, but she didn't stop to fix it. She walked up to him.

"What do you think you're doing?" She was close, but she shouted.

"I need some of my stuff, June. You got the locks changed and I need to get in, that's what I'm doing."

"Get out of here!" She thought of the night they had met, how he had followed her to her car, telling jokes and laughing. "Go away! And don't you dare come to my school again! Don't even think about it."

"I needed the key. That's all, June. I just need to get some of my things." He was using his reasonable voice, the voice of a man with a crazy wife. He held up his hands, to tell her to calm down. She was hysterical. See what he had to put up with? "I need to go inside and get my things." He shrugged. "That's all."

June turned away and waited. She wasn't going to cry. If she was nothing to him, then he was nothing to her either. "There are your things." She stretched her arm out, pointing to the pile on the curb. "I already got them for you."

He looked at the pile standing by the curb. She had kept the stereo and the television set. She had kept the furniture, the dishes, the appliances, the pretty rug that looked almost Persian, the bed, the linen, and the towels. She had given him the old tires and the broken lamp. She didn't care about any of the things they owned, she could get on a bus today and leave everything, but she didn't want him to have any of it. She didn't want him and his girlfriends standing on the carpet that they had found one rainy day at a secondhand store in Alsea. She didn't want another woman

stepping out of the shower and reaching for one of the towels. She didn't want someone else eating from one of her
plates, putting one of her forks between her lips, listening
to music from their stereo, sitting on the same couch, sleeping naked between the same white cotton sheets. She would
rather burn it all.

"I'll be gone in five minutes." He nodded to her hand,
and she looked down at the set of keys she was holding. He
reached for them, but she didn't move. "June," he said,
using the tone she might use with a stubborn child. Her fingers would not let go, and he carefully pried them open. He
got the keys from her, unlocked the door, and went inside.
He had set the newspaper down, and now she picked it up
and sat on the steps, to wait for him to finish.

Later that night it looked like rain, so June went out
with a blue tarp and covered the pile. She tucked everything
in and held it in place with rocks.

Chapter 19

*I*t was May, and the children were making cards for their mothers. In some of the classrooms they had planted flower seeds weeks ago, and now the flowers were almost ready to take home. Mother's Day was a touchy subject. If they didn't have a mother, the children were told a grandmother, aunt, foster mother, or, in a pinch, even a father's girlfriend, would do.

The lunchroom was serving chocolate chip pancakes for breakfast, but the doors didn't open until 7:30. Dozens of kids showed up before then, waiting outside the school, pressed against the doors, motioning for her to let them in early, even though she never did.

At 7:30 she opened the doors, and the kids ran in for breakfast. They were always in a hurry. They ran into the building before school, and they ran out afterward.

"No pushing! Come on, you guys!"

The teachers said *you guys* was sexist, but everybody knew it was gender neutral. Southerners had a perfectly useful way of saying it, *y'all,* but in the north *you guys* had to do.

Cindy hardly ever came in for breakfast, and so June wasn't surprised not to see her on this day.

Missy was helping in the lunchroom, along with Raymond, who hadn't stopped complaining. He didn't see why we had to get up so early. In his other school, class didn't even start until noon. The kids always made outlandish claims about the superiority of their former schools, but when he said the bit about noon, Missy wouldn't just let it go.

She said, "Nuh-uhhh!" and he said, "Uh-huh!" and she said, "Nuh-uhhh!" and he said, "Uh-huh!" and June said, "That's enough!" And they could see that she was right, and grew quiet.

"Cindy got in a fight," said Missy.

The first wave of kids had already been through the line, and now there were only the stragglers. June and Missy and Raymond stood behind the counter waiting. They had piles of chocolate chip pancakes on long aluminum sheets in front of them.

"It was a girl fight," said Missy. "I saw it. With that Claire Hooligan, and Cindy won."

June turned to her. "A fight?"

"A girl fight."

"At school?"

"And now she's suspended."

At eight o'clock the first bell rang, and they were allowed in the rest of the building, but they must not run!

By 8:15 they were expected to be in their classrooms. The problems of tardiness and absenteeism were regular topics at staff meetings. Their parents, if they were lucky enough to have parents, worked nights and slept late; or their parents, or whoever they lived with, left for jobs at the crack of dawn and didn't wake them up. They lived with all kinds of people. They moved often. Sometimes they said good-bye, but sometimes they simply didn't come to school one day.

When June thought of her own situation, she knew it was nothing next to kids without families, kids who could never count on going home to their room or their parents, kids who never belonged anywhere.

After breakfast, she went to the school office. She walked through the gym with its shiny floor and into the long hallway. Her shoes made a loud noise on the floor as she walked. She passed bulletin boards hung with maps of the states and their capitals, drawings of flowers, a chart showing what kinds of pets kids had: dog, cat, hamster, bird, snake, goat, fish.

She went into the office; it was crowded with kids and parents. Parents came in before school sometimes to ask about schedules or lost clothes, medication, lunch money, after-school care, or to tell about problems on the playground or school bus. People act as if the poor don't love their children, June thought, but they do. She thought of all the middle-class specialists whose job it is to document the lives of the poor, and she thought, If we could take their salaries and spend it instead on buying houses, then that would be doing something.

June wasn't in a hurry. She waited in the back of the line, next to two of the school's kindergartners and a nicely dressed woman who held the hand of her young child, preparing, from the looks of it, to ask about fall kindergarten.

"What are you doing in your classroom this week?" June asked the kids, as they waited their turn.

"We're having our mothers in," said one. She was a tiny blonde girl wearing a dress much too large for her, a bow hanging untied in the back.

"I don't have one," said the boy, "but my daddy might come."

"It's fun when mothers or daddies come to school, isn't it?" said June. She turned the blonde girl around and tied the bow that had come undone from her dress.

The nicely dressed woman was watching. Her own child wore a new pink dress with matching tights, patent leather shoes, clean little hands, her hair shiny and pulled back in pigtails.

"Oh, you don't want my daddy to come to school," said the boy. "He's mean."

This was a conversation to head off, but June faltered.

"He made my mom drink gasoline one time!"

"Goodness!" said June. The children were watching her face. They always watched your face at times like this, looking for clues, June assumed, trying to see what people made of such things. "I'm so sorry," said June, "that's sad." She bent forward and told them they didn't have to wait in this big line, and to go on around the counter and talk to the secretary.

When it was her turn, June was told that Cindy had been suspended for three days, and Cindy's teacher, who stood at the photocopy machine, asked if June would mind dropping her schoolwork off, being as she was a friend of the family.

Even though she had told herself she'd never go back, June drove to the Hankses' house that afternoon. She hadn't been there since the night of the birthday dinner. She hadn't been there since she had found out about Bill. She had a morbid mind, and knew what she would think: Bill here in this room, Bill here between these walls, Bill and the dead woman.

These are just thoughts, she told herself, don't worry about them. But she was full of pain. Okay, having a father who makes your mother drink gasoline is a hundred times worse, but what does that mean? she asked herself. Is that supposed to make me feel better?

She turned down the street, where Bill had once turned. Was Cindy's mother his first or had there been other women, all along? She stopped at the Hankses' house. She got out of her car, and the dog across the street at the Santa Claus house barked. It had worn a muddy, nervous path all around the tree where it was tied, and now it pulled against its cord, barking at her. She turned away from it and walked up the steps to Cindy's porch.

She knocked on the door and waited. Louise said to pay attention to the present, period. Look at what is in front of you. She began to name things: a brown door, scratched at the bottom where a dog had wanted in; a black mailbox that made her think of the mailbox she had as a child on McNees Drive. She couldn't imagine not having parents. Being able to count on people, everyone needs that. And see, her mind had drifted off again, to the house where she had lived with her family, a mother, a father, and a brother, and they had dogs and a garden and normal things, a woods to play in, and neighbors. She knocked again. She was going to have to tell her mother about Bill. Brown door, black mailbox, the smell of diesel and someone's burn pile. The dog barking.

What was so good about the present, that we needed to pull ourselves to it constantly?

The door opened and there was Cindy, still in her pajamas. "You're back!" she exclaimed, and she pulled June inside. The house was dark, and the TV was on in the living room.

June stood in the hallway. She had brought Cindy's schoolwork. She had brought a plant that Cindy had grown for her mother, if her mother were alive, a Wandering Jew, but the kids were told to call it Wandering Jewel because Jew wasn't politically correct, although June couldn't imagine why.

Cindy whisked the plant away, as if June might not have seen it, and she asked if June would come for Mother's Day. "Harlan says Mona will be here anyway, if you can't come.

That's his girlfriend." She wrinkled her nose. "Mona," she repeated, as if the name itself were enough explanation. Cindy lowered her voice. "Mona Leadbetter, isn't that a stupid name for someone? But I told him you'd come, see, for dinner. I'm making dinner, and Mona is not invited."

As an adult it was her job to correct bad manners, but June was tired of being an adult. Mother's Day was in four days, and she would have to send her mother something, but she had no money. The phone would be turned off soon, but she didn't need a phone. She didn't need electricity or a car. She didn't need half of what she had.

Cindy was talking about Little Babe. People said old dogs couldn't learn new tricks, but Cindy had taught her to play dead, she said, and she showed June. "Bang!" she said, and Little Babe fell onto her side.

June was thinking of the day her car broke down. She thought of the day of Mr. Pruett. She remembered how she had felt, realizing that she had barely escaped with her life, but now, suddenly, for the first time, she saw that she hadn't gotten away with anything. Her life had ended. Just as surely as if he had strangled her, the life of June Duvall ended that day.

She was thinking these things, but she was smiling, and she heard herself say, "Goodness!" her current expression of amazement. She used to say *Jesus Christ* or *goddamn,* but now she didn't.

"Do you?"

June looked at Cindy.

"Do you like tuna casserole?"

"I love it," said June.

"Cindy!" June was startled to hear another voice in the house. It was a woman. "Cindy, if it's those Jehovah's Witnesses, tell them we don't want any!"

"It ain't the dang Witnesses," Cindy yelled back.

And then the woman appeared. She was scarcely bigger than Cindy, but she moved through the house like she owned it. She came from the direction of Harlan's bedroom, rubbing her face, just waking up. She had bad skin but beautiful large, almond-shaped eyes. She had a natural beauty, but she didn't know what to do with it. She had plucked her dark eyebrows into a thin wavering arch so that she looked both surprised and off-kilter at the same time. She wore too much mascara, and it had smeared around her eyes while she slept. Her hair was badly dyed, a brassy orange color, and the dark roots were showing. All the things that she had done to improve herself had backfired, June thought in that instant before they met, and it seemed like a metaphor, but then seeing metaphors in everything was one of the signs of mental illness, wasn't it?

"My name is June," said June, but, even though she liked to touch people when she met them, she didn't put out her hand this time. She didn't like the other woman here, coming out of Harlan's bedroom, walking around with her brassy hair like she owned the place.

"I heard of you."

"What's *your* name?"

"Mona Leadbetter," said Cindy quickly, stepping forward. "This here is Mona Leadbetter."

June didn't say how do you do or pleased to meet you. She had an irrational urge to grab Ms. Leadbetter by that brassy hair of hers and throw her out the front door. She turned to Cindy. "I want you to keep up with your homework, you hear me? I want you to come back to school on Monday and have everything done."

But Mona wasn't going to be dismissed so easily. "You're that teacher that comes around sometimes, huh," she said. "Harlan says you were friends with Vernay." She gave a little laugh that June could not interpret. "I didn't know she *had* any friends."

"She had lots of friends!" said Cindy.

"Guys." Mona stretched out the word.

"All kinds of friends."

"I know I sure miss her," said June. She was watching the other woman, but she could feel Cindy's eyes on her face. "She was a great friend. There was nobody like her for keeping a secret." June tried to think of other qualities she might mention, things not too far from the truth. "She was always cheerful. She could cheer you up, I'm telling you, and that's important. It's important to have a friend who can make you feel good." The other two were quiet now. They were watching her. She could hear the dog barking across the street. She could hear the TV set on in the living room. "I haven't felt like myself since she died." That was the truth anyhow. "Nothing seems the same." And she started to cry.

"Oh, honey!" said Mona Leadbetter, taking her arm. "I'm sorry." She folded her small arms around June. "I'm so sorry."

I am a hypocrite and a liar, June thought, and it only made her cry harder. She had their sympathy now, but she didn't deserve it. She tried to say *no, forget it,* but Mona told her *let your feelings come out.*

June left as quickly as she could. She was going to stop coming here, she told herself. She'd come once more, on Sunday, Mother's Day, because she had said yes, and she couldn't get out of it. She'd come then, and that would be the last time. It would be closure, like they said in school. They would have closure, things would close up, like a circle, close up and be done. It was a psychological term, maybe, but where had psychology gotten anyone? It was as useless as religion, from what June could tell. June didn't believe in priests or therapists. She was a naysayer. She couldn't help it. No one had the answers. But it was true: a girl needed a mother. That was common sense. What had happened to common sense? What had happened to common decency? Common wasn't good enough for anybody anymore. They all wanted something special. But the point was that Cindy had a mother figure. She had Mona who had put her arm around June and said, "There, there."

She drove home thinking of Mona's arms around her and how you lie sometimes to protect someone. She wondered, When it's not motivated by self-interest, is it still a lie?

Bill's pile stood by the curb, but the blue tarp had come loose from the rocks that held it in place and flapped in the breeze. She got out of her car and approached it. She straightened the tarp where it had folded over and pulled it taut. She anchored the ends, and then she noticed that on the side that faced the street, the neighbor kids had placed a white board. On it they had written, "Property of Bill Duvall. Not for free. Not for sale."

Chapter 20

All over the world people got divorced, and June didn't see how they managed it. Maybe if you had money, you just moved to a new place; put down the security deposit, first and last month's rent; got everything hooked up; hired a moving van; and moved. But people with money, they didn't rent, did they. They went to a realtor and *bought* a new place. They found a house they liked, the right location and size, the right feeling, and they bought it. Maybe if you were rich and getting a divorce, you might even go on a trip to Europe, or at least the Caribbean, and fall in love, if you felt like it.

June couldn't tell how much of her difficulty was due to her economic situation and how much was simply a broken heart. She didn't want a broken heart. Bill didn't have a broken heart, so why should she? Bill was a son of a bitch. The Bill she had known didn't even exist. If her husband Bill had died in a car wreck coming home one night, that would have been better. If he had simply died, then she would still have had the old Bill of her memory, of her past, the beloved Bill, and surely that would have been less of a blow than this.

She had to rewrite her history.

Meanwhile, there was a pink envelope draped around her front doorknob: if she didn't pay her electric bill within two weeks, the electricity would be shut off.

She went inside and sat at the kitchen table.

She could see Bill's pile on the curb, covered with the blue tarp. She wasn't hungry. The phone rang, and she didn't answer it. She sat. Some people in her situation began drinking, but she didn't care enough to drink. She could just sit there and die, she thought, but surely that would take a long time.

Louise had been urging her to go out, have fun, enjoy herself. Overseas, bombs were falling, but here flowers bloomed and sometimes the sun shone. In some countries a person would be happy to walk outside and think her own private thoughts. In some places you'd be happy if someone wasn't cutting your arm off with a machete, or you'd be happy because you weren't hungry, you didn't have cholera, your children weren't dying in your arms. She didn't know how to measure her own distress within the context of the world.

After a while, somebody knocked on the door, but she didn't get up. She couldn't think of anyone she wanted to see. She had heard of crazy people who hid in their houses, who wouldn't answer the phone or the doorbell, who wouldn't go outside even for groceries.

Now the person had moved to the kitchen door, and was knocking on it. "June!" It was his voice. "June! What the hell are you doing?" She shifted her eyes to the door and saw him, peering in through the window at her.

June went to the door and opened it. He came inside and stood in the kitchen next to the stove, and if he had unnecessary, sentimental thoughts, he didn't show it. He said, "Jesus Christ, June, are you all right?"

"I'm just fine."

It was a Thursday, and it occurred to her that he should have left for work by now. He had been going early on Thursdays for some time, but she couldn't think when it had started, although if she looked in her calendar book she'd be able to narrow it down, as if there was still a point to knowing things about him. She wondered if he had a standing Thursday rendezvous. She wondered if he had a secret life that included motels and other men's wives.

He had picked up the mail from her box and was holding it in his hand. "I know this is hard for you, June, and I'm sorry."

She wanted to make a sarcastic remark, but nothing came to mind.

He looked down at the mail in his hands. *Open immediately!* If she wasn't careful they'd turn off her water too. "I never wanted to hurt you," he said, like that meant something. Never wanted, she thought, not like those other men who have affairs. He had never wanted it.

"I guess the point now is, what are we going to do?" he said. He was using his reasonable voice. They were going to have a reasonable conversation, and maybe when they got to the end of it, they would have decided to divorce. That was the next step. Maybe they would have said *we don't need lawyers, not when there is so much trust between us.* Maybe she would have given him everything: the Mercury, the bed, the towels.

June sat back down at the kitchen table, but he didn't join her.

"I know that job barely pays you enough to cover rent," he said. "I know it's not enough to live on."

Maybe in a situation like this, she thought, the most you can hope for is to learn to hate the other person.

"Maybe your mother will help," he said.

Her mother loved Bill.

"Have you told her yet?" he asked. She could feel him looking at her, and then he sighed. "You haven't, have you?"

Bill was not in a position to tell June what to do anymore. She didn't even have to talk to him if she didn't feel like it, and she didn't feel like it now. She didn't want to talk, and she didn't have energy to fight. She was certainly not going to throw herself at his feet, clutching his legs, the way some women would have.

"June, you know I'm not going to leave you high and dry."

She didn't want to think about him anymore. She didn't want him to be so important. She wanted time to think, but she didn't want to think about Bill. She wanted to go someplace quiet, but she didn't know where that would be. Louise kept saying the beach, but the beach wasn't quiet.

The beach in Oregon was stirred up and wild, and it always filled her with longing, and she didn't want longing right now. She wanted a quiet room with a window and a small bed. She wanted someone to make her meals. She wanted to spend her days walking through a garden, not talking. She never wanted to talk again.

Maybe she would be a nun, she thought suddenly, but not a Catholic nun. Maybe she would be some other kind of nun and spend her life in quiet meditation. She didn't want sex anymore, she didn't want to want it, and sex was the main hurdle. She thought about Sean Callahan and how she had secretly loved him, but she hadn't done anything about it because she had already met Bill. Just because you have a feeling doesn't mean you had to do something about it. You can love other people. Everyone does.

Bill was finishing whatever his point had been. He had gotten right to it, but she hadn't been listening. ". . . and we've always gotten along. So I don't see why, if I just sleep on the couch, I can't stay here and, you know, if it doesn't work out I'll leave again. It's to the advantage of both of us—"

"You want to live here?"

"It just makes sense."

"You want to be my roommate, like if I put an ad up and you answered it, like we were strangers?"

"Like we were friends."

"And we'd just act like none of this ever happened?"

"No, June, we'd just act like we're a couple of grown-ups."

She looked away from Bill, out the window, at the blue tarp. "When are you going to get your goddamn things?" she asked, but she said it in a soft voice.

"We'd keep our personal lives separate, June."

She jumped up, went to the door, and flung it open. "Get out of here!"

"You know you can't afford to live here on your own."

The little girl next door had her baby buggy out, and she was pushing it. They would keep their personal lives separate, he said, something he already knew how to do. And she thought of his personal life. She thought of the pretty blonde waitress who had acted so nice to her, who had told her that everything we do, no matter how small, has ramifications. She didn't know who else there was. She didn't know who he was and the life he had. Other people knew things about him that she didn't know. He was her husband, but they had secrets with him.

"Get out of here!" she yelled.

"I know you're upset." He held up his hands to show that he was innocent, but he wasn't innocent. "Just think about it."

"Don't come back here again!"

"Anyway, here's the number where you can reach me." He pointed to a piece of paper with a phone number, lying on the counter, but June couldn't remember him putting it there. She was pushing him out the door.

"Get out!" she yelled again, and saw the little girl next door watching her. She calmed down. He was outside, on the porch. She said to him, in a low and perfectly civil voice, "Take your things."

After he was gone, she thought it was funny how she could want someone here and want him gone at the same time. She gazed at the phone number he had written down and ran her fingers over the writing.

Chapter 21

She was not going to let him bring those things back inside, the things under the tarp. They would have to stay out. Maybe when school was finished, she'd leave. She could live in Portland. She could have boyfriends and date, work in a restaurant and stay up late, cuss when she wanted, and drink after work.

She was sitting at the kitchen table, having toast for dinner, when the phone rang.

"Where the hell have you been?" It was Louise. "I've been calling and calling, and I had a half a mind to get in the car and come over. The baby's sick, or I would have."

"What's wrong with him?"

"It's just a little fever, but you have to be careful with babies."

She was leaning with her back against the wall, looking around. She had done a good job in this kitchen. Everyone liked yellow kitchens, but she had painted hers white, with yellow trim. She had a print of van Gogh's

Sunflowers on the wall, even though Bill had wanted a still life of an apple or bread. Van Gogh had spent his life longing for companionship, but companionship wasn't all it was cracked up to be.

"I can't believe you let Bill back."

"I didn't let him back. He's sleeping in the garage, in his van. It's strictly a financial situation." He could use the bathroom and the kitchen, but he couldn't sleep inside, not even on the couch. He couldn't bring friends home, not even men. She had written the rules on a piece of paper. He hated rules, but everyone had rules. And it was on a trial basis only. If she decided it wasn't working, he had to leave immediately. And the first thing he had to do was go straight to the realtor and pay the rent and the late fee.

"I don't think it's a good idea," Louise said, as if June was in a position to choose only good ideas.

"It's on a trial basis." She had kept the house up while he was gone. She had cleaned everything from top to bottom, the closets, the corners, the windows, all of it, everything. "He'll sleep in the garage and come in through the kitchen." The kitchen was completely clean, even the top cupboards had been washed and organized. You could find anything you were looking for, if it was there. In dreams, houses represent the self. And what about closets? Maybe closets are places where we hide things.

"You could stay here with us," Louise said. "I told you that."

"It will be fine."

"Don't let him sleep with you."

Louise had turned Buddhist, but her husband was Greek Orthodox. They had icons in all the rooms of their house, which meant flat pictures of the Virgin Mary or Jesus. We call Madonna and Elvis icons too, June thought. Now why is that? She moved to the window, with the phone against her ear. Was it her turn to talk?

"I heard Sean is single now," Louise said. "Up in Portland, you know."

June had met Sean one night years before, when he played a gig at the restaurant where she waited tables.

The restaurant had a stage in one corner. The acoustics weren't good, and the bass player complained. The band had fooled around, setting the speakers in one direction and then another, having June listen. June had a good ear.

The band was called Seannie and the Riveters. It wasn't easy waiting tables with the music playing. No one could hear a thing and, besides that, everyone got dreamy. When Sean sang, he made them remember things, and if there was nothing to remember, he made them want. He was a quiet man, Black Irish. Had the black Celtic hair and blue eyes. He stood to the side while he sang, and sometimes he shut his eyes. He was a big tipper and June liked him, but she was in love with the cook so she said no to him. She was never sorry either. She had never regretted it.

That night she went to bed early, but she didn't sleep. She had sleeping pills, but she didn't take them. She lay in bed and waited for the sound of Bill's van outside. She could sense where people were sometimes, and she knew that right now Bill was far away.

When her father died, he had promised that, if he could, he'd come back and give her a message, but he never did. When her father died, she tried to search him out, feeling for him, but she couldn't find him. Her mother felt him sometimes. Her mother, who didn't even believe such things, smelled his tobacco sometimes at night, but when June tried to find him, there was nothing, just an empty place where he had been.

She woke up in the morning, and Bill was in the kitchen. She could feel him there before she got out of bed. Her father was nowhere, but Bill was at the kitchen table. He never got up this early, and she wasn't ready for him yet.

She went to the kitchen in the T-shirt and underwear she had slept in. He had seen it before. He thought she was sexy, but she didn't care about that now. He had made coffee for himself, but not for her, and now she stood at the stove, boiling water.

Once he said that grief didn't suit her, but he said it like this: "You look a lot prettier when you're not crying."

She thought maybe she'd make a list of every bad thing about him. She wouldn't make another list with the good things in it, to be fair, because she didn't have to be fair.

June made her coffee and went into the bathroom to dress for work.

Some women have husbands who beat them, and maybe that makes you set the bar low, she thought. You know a few men like that, and you don't expect much, so you're happy. You say you have a perfect marriage.

She went to work and came home. On Sunday night

she'd have dinner at the Hankses' house. She'd sit at the kitchen table with Mona Leadbetter. She would sit in the chair of the dead woman, the woman who was killed in her place, the woman who had ruined her marriage.

Louise said she should get out more. The baby had been sick, but he was better now, and she wanted to visit. Louise said you have to keep doing the things you enjoy, even if you don't care about them right now, because one day you will care, and you have to keep in the habit. Louise did not understand depression, or whatever this was. Louise with her icons. June didn't even care about Louise. She was jealous of the baby. She was jealous of Louise's husband. June had become a tiny person, like Bill had said.

"You have become a small person," he had yelled at her. He had held his palm down like measuring the height of a young child. "You are a tiny person!" And then later, he had tried to joke about it. They used to laugh about their fights, and he didn't understand that you don't laugh now, when the fight doesn't end. It was just one long fight now, everything figured into the balance sheet, and they would never again get to the part where they could joke about it.

When Bill came home that night, she woke up and looked at the clock. He had come straight home after work this time. She heard the van, and, after a while, she heard him inside the house. It was a small house, and he was in the kitchen, and then he was in the hallway.

He was at her bedroom door, but the door was locked. She could hear the knob, when he tried to turn it. Yogi Berra said that when you get to a fork in the road, you should take it, and this was a fork in the road, maybe, but she didn't move. Her clothes were hot against her body, and she wanted to throw the blankets away from her.

The window was open and a little breeze blew in. She thought she could smell honeysuckle, but surely it was too early for that. She had been dreaming she had a baby, and she was taking her to church. Everyone was singing, but she couldn't remember the baby's name. Alice? Lily? A baby is a new beginning, but what does it mean when you forget the name?

Bill was knocking softly. "June," he said, just loud enough for her to hear. Maybe if she opened the door and forgave him, he'd be different from now on, and it would be the beginning of their new life together, but she doubted it. "June, are you awake?" He had a good, deep, sexy voice. She wanted to open the door, but she wasn't like him, giving in to everything she wanted just because she wanted to. The light from the streetlamp came in through the window, and she held her hand open so that it shone on her palm.

The next night he came home late, and he was drunk. She could tell by the way he moved around the kitchen. He drank too much. He had big ideas, but he didn't do anything about them. He felt sorry for himself. He was an egotist. He complained. He was jealous of her, but he pretended not to be. He said he wanted her to go out, have a good time, but really he wanted her home. He didn't like the same movies she liked. He didn't read books, except cookbooks. He wanted his own restaurant, but he wasn't willing to work for it. He didn't know any of his own faults, and if she told them to him, he wouldn't recognize them. He only knew her faults and the faults of the people around him. How could she have ever loved him?

She had come to a fork in the road, and she had done nothing, and in doing nothing she had taken it. Her father used to love Yogi Berra. He had a book of his quotes in the bathroom. Her father used to sit on the toilet and smoke Raleighs and read Yogi Berra. She wondered what kind of husband he had been, and she marveled at the fact that so many women have husbands. She'd never do that again, she told herself. She was a man-hater now.

On Saturday, she wore the dead woman's yellow linen skirt. She had no reason to dress up, but she put the skirt on and went to the kitchen where Bill sat. She had meant to wash it, but she hadn't gotten around to it. Bill was at the kitchen table, and she went to the refrigerator. Her appetite was coming back. She could feel him watching her, from behind. He always wanted what he couldn't have, or maybe he was thinking of the skirt.

"Going someplace special?" he asked.

She didn't answer. She poured cereal into a bowl and sat across from him at the table. From where he sat, he could look out the window and clearly see his pile of things on the sidewalk. "The tarp's come loose again," she said, pointing with her spoon.

"Why the hell did you do that?" he asked, but she wasn't answering any questions. "Lookit"—he jabbed his finger at the window—"it's falling all over the sidewalk."

"Yeah, and you better move it before the blind girl

comes by and falls over it." She wanted to add "you big son of a bitch" at the end, but she didn't. She used to get mad at the parents for fighting in front of their kids and hating each other, but now she could see how it happened.

Across from her, he ate his eggs and toast. First, he cut all the food on his plate into bite-size pieces with his knife, even though it was just eggs, and you could use your fork and cut as you go, which is the way you were supposed to eat eggs anyway. His fork hit the plate with every bite and when he bit into the toast it sounded like someone held an amplifier to his mouth. How had she ever loved him?

She stood up and got the ironing board out of the closet. She set it up in the kitchen, took off her blouse, and began to iron. Maybe she'd go downtown today, or maybe she'd go to Louise's.

She had on the dead woman's yellow bra, and Bill watched her. Yellow, the color of forgetfulness. In another month her yellow roses would bloom, but where would she be in a month? She didn't look at Bill, but she stood facing him. Most men might not notice a woman's skirt or under-wear, but Bill would. Still, how could he be sure? Had he seen these things on June, he would be thinking, and gotten mixed up? How many women were there, and could he keep them all straight? Did he see them at WinCo and search his memory for a name? What is the point of a rela-tionship? What is the point if you lie? June bent forward. He had always loved her breasts.

Chapter 22

On Mother's Day she drove to the Hankses' house to eat dinner with Cindy and Harlan and, presumably, Mona Leadbetter. She wasn't dressed up this time. She wore blue jeans and a T-shirt. She pulled her hair back in a plain ponytail. She didn't wear the fancy yellow bra, and she didn't wear her favorite boots.

She parked in front of the house and, in a last-minute concession to vanity, adjusted the rearview mirror and put lipstick on. She thought it was strange that she looked just the same as ever. She thought of Mikey, after his mother left, and she remembered looking at him, expecting something different, some change, some sign, but he had looked just the same as ever. He had looked like any other nine-year-old boy.

She got out of the car and went to the door, and when Cindy opened it, she walked inside.

She was not nervous this time, although she wasn't looking forward to dinner with Ms. Leadbetter, an unnecessary concern, as it turned out. Harlan and Mona were going to Teddy's Bar and Grill, on a date, Mona explained, and Cindy could have June to herself. June had hardly gotten in the door when Mona launched into her explanation.

"Teddy is my cousin. Just got out of rehab. Well, first he tried to shoot himself in the head, at one of those rest areas out on the interstate. He had his girlfriend with him, and they were in a fight. So he pulls out his gun and he's gonna shoot himself right in the temple." Mona pointed to her own temple by way of illustration. "But he's got this old shoulder problem, his rotar cuff, you know, from throwing hardballs. He was big on baseball, so he's got that rotar cuff problem, and couldn't get his arm up high enough, and so what he did was he blew out his, you know, his sinus cavity, his nose I guess you'd call it. Just blew it out. He always had a temper, that whole side of the family does. And then, of course, he got in the drugs again." Mona laughed. "No snorting this time, if you know what I mean." She lowered her voice. "He got into the bad stuff—but then he went to rehab, and now he's bought himself a little bar. Isn't that right, Harlan? He's got himself a bar named after him and everything, and tonight is the grand opening, ennit, honey?"

June shifted her eyes to Honey, and he nodded. In the movies women are attracted to bad boys, but they are Marlon Brando or Bruce Willis. They are the male version of the librarian who tears off her glasses and you discover that she is a knockout—only instead of being secretly gorgeous, the men are secretly heroic. The men, at great personal risk, defy all odds, overcome adversity, and rescue the woman. But in real life a man like Harlan wasn't anything more than what you saw—and his female counterpart was someone like Mona, who hadn't stopped talking once.

"We appreciate you coming over and all," Mona continued.

We, we, we. This is the way she talked, as if she had a right to him.

"Cindy can stay alone, now she's ten years old. That's what I tell Harlan. I was babysitting when I was ten, but he is so goddamn protective. He was before too. Before this business with Vernay. Not that it got him anywhere. You can't help things, sometimes, I tell him. You feel better when you got an adult around, course not just any adult. We had a guy used to come around here, guy name of Larry, who Harlan always stuck up for, but something didn't seem quite right to me, come to find out he was abusing little girls." She leaned close to June, and June could smell her perfume and her cigarettes. "Sexually," she said.

"But he never bothered Cindy," Harlan was quick to say.

Cindy was standing right there, and she shook her head, agreeing.

The last time June was here, Harlan had led her into the living room. She had waited on the couch while he showered. She had thought he was special, but she was just lonely. She wanted someone to rescue her. She wanted to fall in love, maybe she wanted to punish Bill. Now she stood in the doorway, still holding her pocketbook, thinking how little she understood people—how little she understood even herself. It would be one thing if people were driven by simple self-interest, but human psychology was much more complicated than that.

"Let her get in the door, would you," said Harlan, finally. He put his hand on June's arm, leading her into the living room.

"Cindy made spaghetti for you," he said.

"From a can," added Mona.

"And there's French bread and salad."

"He had to get *special* bread from a bakery," said Mona. Apparently the bread was a point of contention, and now she frowned at Harlan.

"Cindy's been so excited," Harlan told June.

That night after dinner, Cindy put in a movie, and they sat in the living room to watch it. Cindy made popcorn. They didn't talk about Mother's Day, but Cindy did give her a card that said, "To My Good Friend, June," and she gave her the plant from school, the Wandering Jew, which she called Jewel. They sat in the living room with the animals. Cindy had put a dress on Little Babe, and Little Babe sat on the couch between them. Cindy piled pillows up in front of them because this was a scary movie and who knew when they'd need to duck behind something. Cindy held the gerbil named Marge on her lap and, because she didn't want to leave anyone out, she got the fishbowl and set it on the table.

They watched an old movie called *The Premature Burial*,

about a man who had a disease that made him appear dead when he wasn't. The movie was set in the days before embalming, and the man was buried alive. Later, when his coffin was opened up, there were marks on it where he had clawed at the lid.

After the movie, they went outside to sit on the front porch. When June was a little girl, back in Greenville, she'd sit out front with her mother and her brother, and the neighbor kids might come, and they'd catch lightning bugs. They'd tear the wings off and make wedding rings with those bugs, because they didn't know any better. They'd put the lit-up bodies of the dying lightning bugs on their faces or on the dog's nose with not the slightest guilt, and the funny thing, June had always thought later, was the fact that all this time her mother sat beside them, drinking iced tea and saying nothing.

"What's your favorite thing to eat?" Cindy asked her, but she didn't wait for an answer. "I like spaghetti, but not the way Mona fixes it with the noodles all stuck together. I like Mexican food. Mona says she can make Mexican, but all she knows is tacos. Anybody can make tacos. You get the hamburger, you know, with lettuce and tomatoes."

"And cheese," said June.

"I like chicken enchiladas, but Mona says they're too hard."

"Chicken enchiladas? They're not hard."

"See that house over there?" Cindy pointed to the house across the street, the house with the plastic Santa and the dog that barked. "Vernay hated that guy there. After his wife left then he stopped paying the garbage man. He just threw his garbage outside, and then there were rats. There were real rats. Vernay saw them."

"He threw his garbage in the yard?"

"When she saw that, Vernay went over to talk to him. She hates rats. She never even liked Marge, but I don't think a gerbil is even close to a rat." Cindy paused for a moment before continuing. "He is real mean to his dog, that dog over there. It's a rottweiler and people say rottweilers are mean. We had a pit bull once, and it was the nicest dog you ever seen. People are mean to dogs, and then the dogs get mean, and they put them to sleep—they call it *put to sleep,* but it really means kill them. They kill so many dogs down at the pound. Did you know that? I read about it, and then Vernay said it was true."

"It's sad," agreed June.

They sat quietly for a moment, and then Cindy asked, "How did they know my mom was really dead?"

Her mother's body had been found in the woods, beneath leaves and dirt.

"They can tell now if someone is dead or not."

"They burnt her up."

"They embalm dead bodies now, and so if you're not already dead, you die then. They take the blood out." June smoked a cigarette, even though Cindy was a student, and she was supposed to set a good example. She drank a beer. Cindy sat beside her, with Little Babe on her lap. Little Babe was a good sport. She sat quietly in her dress.

"What did you like best about her?" Cindy asked.

June took a deep breath. "Well," she said, "she was so pretty. Your mother was the prettiest thing I ever saw. She had such a sweet face. And your mother, she loved you so much."

"She still does!" exclaimed Cindy. "That's what Harlan says."

"Of course she does. She loves you like an angel now, and angels love in a perfect way. People can't help but get mad sometimes, or forgetful, but angels are never mad, and they are always mindful. They have good memories, and they are completely pure because they don't have to run around down here anymore, worrying about rent money and the like. She is smiling down on you every minute." June paused, and then she asked, "Can you feel her sometimes?"

June had felt the presence of Cindy's mother. When was that? Was it the first time she came here? Was it the second? She had felt her the way you feel someone in the room with you when the lights are out. Like she could hear her breathe, like if she reached over, she might touch her arm, like any minute she might hear her whisper.

June said, "I can feel my father. I can smell his tobacco. He smoked a pipe, and sometimes at night I can smell that pipe." But that was wrong; her mother had been the one to smell the pipe.

"Why do pipes smell good, but cigarettes smell bad?" asked Cindy.

"I'm not sure," said June, and she blew the smoke away from the girl.

"I can feel her right now," said Cindy. "Can you?"

June sat quietly for a moment. They were on the front steps of the house. Across the street, the dog had stopped barking, and it was quiet, but lights were on. She could hear traffic from a few blocks away, a horn, a motor. She could hear a baby crying from one of the houses, but it was faint. She didn't want to feel the presence of the woman who had destroyed her life. Just because someone is dead doesn't mean they were good.

"What else did you like about her?" asked Cindy.

"She always looked on the good side of things. I guess that's why I liked her so much. I'm not like that. I see the bad, I can't help it, I see what's bad, but she would always make me see the goodness in things, the funny part—you know? She could make me laugh about anything."

Cindy laughed out loud, thinking of this, and she exclaimed, "Isn't that the truth! Oh, she was so funny. She was the funniest person I ever met. She could of gone on the TV and had her own show."

"Whenever I was down in the dumps," said June, "she could pull me right out."

"Little Babe is like that."

"We had this joke," June said, looking up at the sky. "When I would complain about something, my job—"

"Your job at school?" Cindy was surprised.

June shrugged. "Sometimes things get to you. Anyhow, I'd start to complain and your mom, she'd say, 'It don't matter,' she'd say it in this certain voice, and we'd laugh."

And Cindy imitated that voice, saying, "It don't matter."

June stood up, stepped off the porch, and walked to the sidewalk in front of them. She threw her cigarette butt down, but she was barefoot, and didn't step on it. "Let's get you to bed," she said.

June hadn't been in the bedroom since she had found out the truth about Cindy's mother. She hadn't been there since the day she had taken the clothes. She thought of Bill, watching her from the kitchen table as she ironed her blouse, leaning forward, in the dead woman's lacy yellow bra. *Come here, June,* he had said. *Come here, baby.* He was used to getting his way, but she had ignored him.

She tucked Cindy into bed, and stood looking down at her. Even though June had sworn this would be the last visit, she heard herself say, "Next time, I'll make enchiladas for you."

"Chicken enchiladas?"

"If that's what you want."

"When?"

"Go to sleep."

She kissed Cindy good night and turned to leave, but the girl called out, "Stay 'til I'm asleep. Please? My uncle does, if I ask him to."

"He stays?"

"He tells me stories. He knows good ones!"

June sat on the other bed, the dead woman's bed, and she tried to think of a story. "What stories does Harlan tell?"

"Superman stories, you know, about kryptonite and flying and rescuing people. It's got Lois Lane too. But I heard all them. Tell me something different."

"Once upon a time," June said. She sat on the edge of the bed, barely touching it, watching the shape of the girl across from her. "There were three bears."

"Oh, not that one! That's a baby one!" Cindy hesitated. "Tell me a story about my mom."

June was quiet. Her legs were pulled close to her body, and now she stretched them out. She needed to relax. She needed to calm down. She would tell a story, and any minute Cindy would sleep. She'd go downstairs and watch TV, and eventually Harlan and Mona would come back. Harlan and Mona. She thought of Harlan, waiting by the front door, with his clean white shirt, his blue jeans and shiny brown boots. He had wet his hair and combed it back, and he had shaved, and he had done all these things for Mona who never stopped talking. She thought of them in bed. She thought of Mona facing the ceiling, her arms around his neck, her skin pressed against his white sheets, talking and talking. She thought of the skin on his face and how it must feel.

"Tell me!" said Cindy.

"You tell me a story," June countered.

"About what?"

"I don't know. Anything." She paused. "Tell me a story about your friend Bill."

"Do you know Bill?" Cindy's voice was surprised.

"No," said June quickly, "I met him the other day at school. Remember?"

"And you were so mean."

"I was just doing my job."

"Bill is nice."

June didn't trust her voice to speak. She sat back on the bed, blinking, while the girl was quiet, thinking how nice Bill was, she supposed.

"Don't you think he's handsome?"

June turned to lie down. She put her head on the pillow, facing the ceiling.

"They were going to get married."

June wanted to say, *Stop, that's enough,* but she didn't.

"And then he would adopt me, and I'd get his name and everything."

June lay very still, holding her breath. She could feel her heart pounding. She could hear the blood in her ears. Across the street, the dog began to bark furiously. She could imagine him, pulling against his cord. "When did you first meet Bill? Was it a long time ago?"

"And I was going to be the flower girl and maybe Lural could too. You can have more than one flower girl. I never did it before, but Lural did, for when her sister got married."

"Did you know him last Christmas?"

"Bill? Sure, he got me Marge, with her cage and everything. He wanted to get me a turtle, you know the kind, comes with a little palm tree, but my mom says they make you sick."

"Did you know him last summer?"

"What I really want is a horse, you know."

June put her hand on the bed beside her, her fingers outstretched. "Did he come here, to this room?"

"Why are you so nosy about Bill?" asked Cindy, annoyed. "He wasn't even at her funeral."

June rolled onto her side and looked at the shadow that was Cindy, beside her. "Maybe he didn't know," she said.

"June," said Cindy, in a small voice, "what makes someone kill someone else?"

"I don't know."

June lay on the dead woman's bed for a long time after Cindy fell asleep. She lay facing the ceiling. She'd never come back here again. She didn't care if, in a weak moment, she'd promised to make one of Cindy's favorite meals. She was finished, and this was closure. The plant and Mother's Day, the dinner, sitting on the front porch, the movie, and here, this, it was all closure, and now it was closed. If Cindy needed a mother figure, she had Mona who couldn't be any worse than the mother herself.

She kept thinking of Bill, here. She couldn't move past it. Bill, in this room. Bill with Cindy's mother. Cindy's mother would be lying right about here, where I am, facing the ceiling with her pretty little smiling, generous, always-ready-to-laugh, always-look-on-the-good-side-of-things, ready-to-do-anything-for-anybody face. Bastard, she thought, he could have at least gone to the funeral.

Chapter 23

June went downstairs at midnight, to wait for Harlan and Mona. She waited on the couch, but the TV was off. She hadn't brought a book, and so she simply waited. She wasn't going to think about Bill anymore. She had thought of him enough. There was Bill, and there was the other Bill. The Bill with secret thoughts. The Bill making arrangements, making plans and promises to someone else. She'd never forgive him. Her principal said that resentment was a hot burning coal you hold in your hands, and you need to drop it, drop that hot burning coal, but she wasn't going to drop it.

She got up and walked around the house. She wasn't going to snoop. Some people would have looked in drawers, but June didn't. She went to the kitchen and looked out the window. She rinsed her face in the sink. She opened the refrigerator and closed it. She opened a cupboard and found a bottle of whisky, poured herself a little glass, and sat down at the kitchen table. She and Cindy had done the dishes and cleaned up.

She wished she was someone like Mona, simple and obvious, but with good taste. She wondered what Harlan and Mona were doing now. Were they dancing? Were they sitting on bar stools with his hand on her leg?

June put her palm down flat on the table and spread her fingers out. She wouldn't mind being alone. Sean Callahan was single again, but she didn't want Sean. She missed sex, but women can always find sex. She finished the whisky, poured herself another glass, and walked toward the living room. It wouldn't hurt if she peeked in Harlan's room, she told herself.

June stood in his doorway, looking in. She flipped the light switch on the wall just inside the door, but nothing happened. She went into the room and found a lamp sitting on a small table by Harlan's bed. She turned it on and looked around.

It was a small room, hardly large enough to hold the bed and dresser. The bed was not made, but the covers were pulled up. The closet door was shut. A pair of panty hose lay on the floor. June opened the closet door. She touched the shirts with her hand and then smelled that hand. She looked down at his shoes on the floor of the closet. After her father died, the saddest thing of all was the sight of his shoes, sitting by the door. Until that moment, she hadn't believed he was dead. It was funny, June thought, how our humanity reveals itself in these odd things, somebody's shoes, or a bed left unmade. She closed the closet door.

There were books on the table by his bed: a mystery, a book about the history of Iraq, and a manual for working on diesel engines. She sat on the bed and opened the history book to the section on the Ottoman Empire. June had just begun to read when she heard a noise outside. She listened carefully, holding her breath, and then stood up and went to the window, pulled the Venetian blind aside, and peeked out. It was just a neighbor. It was not Harlan and Mona coming home—coming home to this room where they would undress and climb between the sheets, put their heads on the pillows, and turn to each other, maybe. She looked at the bed.

In high school Nancy Kindig would invite boys to visit while she babysat, and while the kids slept, she would have sex. Once you did something like that, how could you restrain yourself in other ways? She thought suddenly of soldiers coming home after they killed people. She thought of Ralphie's father. She thought of Bill and the women he slept with. Once you cross a line, how do you get back?

She put the book on the table and straightened the bed where she had sat. There were kids at school who seemed to have no barrier between a thought and an action, nothing holding them back, no restraints, no boundary lines keeping them on the inside with everyone else. June turned off the light, hesitated, picked up a pillow, and went back to the living room.

She sat on the couch. It was a warm night, and she was getting sleepy. She lay down with her cheek on his white pillow.

· · ·

She woke up when he came into the room. She watched him moving quietly, trying not to wake her. He sat on the chair next to her and took off his brown boots, then he leaned back in the chair and looked at her. It took a moment for him to see that she was awake, watching him. She could see his eyes in the dim light, and his white T-shirt. She could hear his breath. They watched each other. She could see his eyes blinking. They waited and then finally she slid over, making room, and he moved from the chair to the small space she had made for him. She put her hand on his back, and he leaned forward to kiss her. He put his hand on her cheek. He moved his fingers under her chin. He tasted her lips with his tongue. He lay down beside her, his legs pressed against her legs, his hips against her hips, his hand on her face, on her soft throat, on her ears, and on her eyelids, and all the time she didn't say a word, and he didn't say a word, but sometimes they sighed. June pulled off her shirt and threw it on the floor. Sometimes a thought would come to her. What if Cindy wakes up? What about tomorrow? What about the girlfriend? What if he gives me something? What if I get pregnant? But those were tiny, pale thoughts, when they were set beside this other thing, and she was moved along and forgot them all.

Chapter 24

"Y̶ou were late last night," said Bill the next morning. It was a Monday, but it was teacher planning day, and there was no school. She slept late, and now stood at the sink, making coffee, in her robe. June had wondered about this moment, the night before, thinking she would regret what she had done, but she didn't regret it. She felt like a girl. She felt like she was someone who, without knowing it, had fallen into a long and terrible sleep, but everywhere that Harlan had been, he had left a trail of wakefulness.

"Where were you?" Bill sat at the kitchen table with the newspaper open in front of him. He had eaten breakfast, and the plate was pushed to one side. "It's your own business, I know that. I don't care where you go or who you go with. I don't care what you do, June. It's not my business and you don't have to answer to me, that's not the point. The point, June, is simple consideration, that's all—thinking of the other guy. A little phone call is all I needed, a note, something. I come home and you're not here and what do you think is the first thing I think now, after what's happened? What do you think? After what happened to Vernay?"

She heard the name without flinching. She stood at the counter drinking her coffee. She was going to say something sarcastic, but she didn't want an argument yet. She was in a state of pleasure, and she wasn't ready to leave it. "Sorry," she answered, but she wasn't sorry. He had lain on the couch with her, and he had taken his time. He had not been nervous or hurried or selfish. He had not rushed forward. He had put his fingers in her mouth, and she had kissed them.

"I thought maybe they got the wrong guy and now he's grabbed you too. I thought, next thing I know I'll get a call from the police."

"I said I'm sorry."

"It's just common consideration."

She sat down at the kitchen table across from Bill. Outside the blue tarp had come loose, and she looked at it, but she didn't say anything. Harlan had slid his hand under her.

"Want some eggs?"

"No." She could feel Harlan's breath on her neck. She could feel the weight of him, his skin on her skin, the bones of his hips.

Bill turned the page of the newspaper. "If you ask me, we've got the beginning of another Vietnam on our hands."

Maybe it didn't mean a thing, she told herself. People have sex with each other, and then they carry on like usual, and the sex is just part of their history together like going to a rock concert or spending a nice day at the beach. Only this wouldn't be a nice day at the beach. It would be the day a comet hit, but not the kind of comet that killed the dinosaurs. It would be a day you rode whales, a day you swam with porpoises. And she wondered how something so normal, sex, could be so extraordinary. She wished she could talk about it, but there was nothing to say, and she wondered, fleetingly, if it was like this for Bill and the other women, but then she thought no, it wouldn't be like this for him. She felt that she had a great unspeakable secret, and then she heard the doorbell.

Bill got right up and went to the door. She heard him open it, and she leaned forward to look out the window. She saw Harlan's car sitting at the curb, but it was too late. She heard them at the front door, asking each other confused and angry questions. What was Bill doing here? What was Harlan doing here? She stood up, but it was too late now.

On top of the men's voices, she heard Cindy. "It's the wrong place, I'm telling you. You got Bill's place. We stopped here before, like I said, Uncle Harlan. She doesn't live here. She doesn't live here. This here is Bill's place." She kept saying it, like saying it would make it true. "It's Bill's."

Cindy's voice came from the front porch, but Harlan had stepped inside.

"Is that where she was last night?" Bill demanded. "Was she with you? Oh, for God's sake!" And then he turned to call her. "June!"

June could hear Cindy's high-pitched voice: "Let's just go!"

She pulled the robe around her and went to the front hallway, where they waited, with their heads turned, watching her. She put one foot in front of the other. It seemed hard to walk, as if her feet had suddenly gotten too small to support her body. She wanted to hold on to the wall, but she didn't. She walked toward them, and they waited, silent and, it seemed to her, hopeful. And then she stood with them, and still they waited. She thought of the quiet place that's inside each of us and available anytime we look for it. But June couldn't find that quiet place.

"Why are you here?" cried Cindy, and Harlan told her, "Be quiet!" but she wasn't quiet. She yelled at June, "You said you didn't know him. You said you didn't!"

June looked from Cindy to Harlan. He had dressed up and shaved. He had on a clean pressed blue shirt the color of his eyes. "We thought we'd take you for breakfast," he said. And everyone was quiet for a moment, thinking of this innocent idea.

June untied her robe and tied it again, tighter.

Then Harlan asked, "What's he doing here?"

"I'm her goddamn husband! That's what I'm doing here. I live here."

"Not anymore," said June, quickly. She turned to Harlan and to Cindy, "He's not my husband anymore." And then she added, "It isn't what it looks like." But what did it look like? It looked like a bunch of lies, that was the first thing. She wanted to take Harlan aside, privately, and tell him the story, beginning with the newspaper article, or no, the day the fuel pump went out, on Jackson Street named after Andrew Jackson who had worn the skins of dead Indians for a belt.

Harlan began to shout. He said he didn't know what kind of fucked-up thing they had going. He didn't know what they were up to. What did they want?

They were all shouting.

"Vernay was a real special lady," Bill shouted over Cindy's voice.

It was like a tangled-up piece of wire, June thought, and if she could just grab hold of one part of it, she might be able to work her way back to the beginning, when Vernay was killed instead of her.

Out of the confusion of their voices, she heard Bill. "She didn't even know Vernay," he said, and now there was stunned silence. They froze, and then they turned, looking at her in this new light. Even Cindy was quiet now. June watched helplessly, seeing herself diminish in their eyes. She could see herself turned into something false and monstrous, something conniving and mean, and she wanted to stop it, but couldn't think how.

"You made it all up!" said Cindy, but now her voice was an angry whisper.

"I just wanted to help you."

"You made it all up. You didn't even know her." Now there were only the lies she had told. Lie upon lie. The clothes she had taken. The stories she had told. Now Cindy could go back and rewrite their history, and Harlan could rewrite it too.

"I'm so sorry," she said. "I only wanted to help you."

"Help us?" said Harlan. "Help us?"

"You were just telling a bunch of lies!" shouted Cindy, launching herself toward June.

Harlan grabbed the girl and said, "Shut up!" And she did shut up. She shut up and held still, crying, while Harlan came up close to June, face-to-face, and he said, "You stay away from us. You stay away from Cindy, and you stay away from me. You stay away. We don't want nothing to do with you, period, you hear me?" But talking got him worked up. "There is something wrong with you," he said. The night before, she had slid over, and he had lain next to her. He had put his hand under her and lifted her toward him. "You only wanted to help? I'll tell you how you can help. You can help by leaving us alone, that's how you can help. You can help by staying away." He took hold of Cindy, and they moved toward the door. "Just stay away from us."

Chapter 25

June spent the day in her room with the door locked. The window was open, and she could hear the neighborhood children outside, arguing. Sometimes Bill knocked. "Let's talk," he would say. He pressed his mouth against the door. "June!" But she didn't have anything to say to him. She thought of the stories she had told Cindy about her mother and the questions she had asked about Bill the night before, and she knew the girl would be remembering these same things in this new light and would hate her for them.

"Dinner's in the refrigerator," Bill said, at last. He didn't move away, and she could feel him there, his body pressed against the door, waiting.

He was the one who had told, she reminded herself. He had said, "She didn't even know Vernay." How much better if she had been able to tell it herself, to think of the first thing to say and then the next, to make a story out of it, with a beginning, one thing leading to the next, but instead to save himself he had taken the worst part and flung it out.

"I'm going to work—dinner is in the refrigerator, June."
She heard him try the door again. "Baby," he said, "come
on, baby, open the door."

She walked to the door and opened it. She didn't care
what she looked like. She hadn't brushed her hair yet, but
she was dressed. She needed a bath. She needed to wash her
face in cold water and have something to eat. She wanted a
cigarette.

He stood in the doorway, looked at her. He had combed
his hair back from his face, the way she liked it. He had
dressed in his good black pants.

"It doesn't matter what they think, June," he said.
Encouraged by her silence, he added, "It's just you and me
now." He was standing close enough for her to hear when
he whispered, "That's what you want, isn't it?"

She looked down at his shoes and thought, Even today
he hasn't forgotten to polish them.

Maybe if she could arouse her own anger, it would be
better, but they had never learned to fight. They were not
fighters. They got along. They were not combative people,
and they did not often shout at each other. Had they
shouted lately? He had shouted that she was small, like
small was bad. If they could shout, truly shout, and break
things, if she could throw dishes, or furniture, if she could
smash his windshield and throw herself on him, scratching
and biting, maybe it would be better. Maybe something
would be worked out. At least, she thought, it would be
honest. But in the end, she simply stood looking at him,
feeling his otherness, if there was such a word, feeling that

he was not her twin. He was not her husband. He was not even someone she recognized. Maybe if she saw him on the street, there would be the vague sense of having seen him someplace before, and that's all.

He stood in the doorway smiling.

"Thank you for the dinner," she said.

After he had left, she sat on the edge of her bed and looked out the window. The phone rang, but she didn't answer. It was a warm evening, almost summer. When she was a girl, June would be gone all day, playing in the woods, but children weren't allowed to play alone now.

They were watched all the time. They rode their bicycles in circles from the sidewalk in front of their house to the street, to the sidewalk of the house across from them, or they sat inside. They had babysitters or they went to activities. They never had a minute to themselves. She thought about all the neighborhoods that appeared childless, and of the buses and downtown streets empty of unescorted children. She thought of the scandalous way parents were talked about, if they let their children walk the streets unaccompanied, if they left them alone in their houses or in their neighborhoods. Did the children know what they were missing? Were they ever tempted to break free of their mothers' protection, to pedal down the street or across town, go down to the river alone, make secret forts in the weeds, stay out all night?

At nine, the doorbell rang. She looked out the window and saw Harlan's car parked in front of her house. The bell rang again and now there was pounding. She knew that the thoughts she had as she hurried to the door were stupid and irrational, but that didn't stop them from coming. She thought, He understands now, and he's forgiven me. It was all just a terrible mistake. He was sorry. No, she would say, I'm the one who's sorry. She would put her hand over his mouth. No, it's me that's sorry. She would feel his lips beneath her palm.

But as soon as she saw his face, it was clear that Harlan had not come to make amends. "Have you seen Cindy?" he shouted and, reading the answer from her face, he added, "I don't know where she is! I can't find her. She's gone. She's just gone."

June thought of the kids in the lunch line. She's gone missing, they had said, but she'd only been home with Harlan.

"Gone? What do you mean, she's gone?"

"She hasn't come back," he said, and now he looked behind June, into her house, but clearly Cindy wasn't there. This was the last place she'd be. "She left, you know she cried all morning in her room. She cried the whole fucking morning in there." He waited for June to say something, and when she didn't, he added, "And now she's run away!"

It had started to drizzle, but Harlan stood on her porch in his shirtsleeves. The neighbor kids had gone inside. The blue tarp covering Bill's things had been loose earlier, but someone had fixed it.

"Run away from home?" Surely she was too young to run away from home, June thought. "When did you last see her?"

"She left about two o'clock."

"Where was she going?"

"I don't know where she went, that's the point."

"Have you called the police?"

"The police?"

"Yeah," she said. "The police, the police, have you called the police?"

"I'm not calling the police."

June stepped aside so Harlan could come in, but he stayed where he was. She could hear the engine of his car, still running. "I'm sure there's a logical explanation for this." June worked at a school, and she knew that when a child couldn't be found there was almost always a simple explanation that did not involve anything disturbing. She's probably at a friend's house."

"I checked with everybody!" he shouted.

"What about Mona?"

But he didn't need June to do his thinking for him. He turned to leave. His car was still running, and now he ran from her porch, down the steps, to the sidewalk, to his car, got inside, slammed the door, and drove away.

Had he checked the neighbors? Had he looked in the park? Had she taken money or extra clothes? Did she have Little Babe with her? June thought of Ralphie Pruett's father and other men like him. There's a logical explanation, she reminded herself. Like at school, when they can't find a child. When she first started working at the school, she panicked every time a child was missing, but soon she had realized they were simply in the wrong room, they had sneaked outside to play on the tire swing, they had left with a babysitter, gone to the nurse, taken the wrong bus. There were so many logical explanations. Hardly any children were stolen and killed. They were at a friend's house, that was all. They were at the mall. They were someplace safe, surrounded by adults who were not crazy.

She got the keys and ran outside to her car, and then she drove to the Hankses' house. It was raining, but she had forgotten her jacket. She hadn't brushed her hair yet. She drove too fast, and when she got there she parked, ran up the steps to the house, threw the door open, and went inside. It occurred to her suddenly that Mona Leadbetter might be here, but almost at once she found Harlan alone, in the kitchen, hanging up the phone. He didn't seem surprised to see her.

"The only thing I can hope is she's with Mona, but I haven't been able to find Mona either."

"You mean you haven't talked to Mona? Harlan, that's where she is—she's with Mona, that's all."

"But Mona's not around."

"What do you mean?"

"Her brother told me she's not even in town right now."

"What about her friend, Lural?"

"I've called her friends."

June sat down at the kitchen table. Children do disappear sometimes, she knew that, and maybe this is the way it started. Maybe you wait around thinking of logical explanations and one by one they are proven wrong. "I still don't see why you won't call the cops."

"Lookit, will you shut up about the cops? I'm not calling them, period."

She started to remind him that he hadn't called the cops
when his sister disappeared either, but she stopped herself.
She said, "Maybe she's at the park."

"I drove by there."

"Maybe she went with Mona."

"She doesn't even like Mona."

"She's probably just at somebody's house—"

"I told you I called every friend she has."

"Why don't you call Mona again?"

"She doesn't have a phone. I went there twice already
and talked to Sam, that's her brother, I talked to him."

June looked at the clock. She thought of what had happened to Cindy's mother, and she thought, What are the
odds of the same thing happening to Cindy? The odds are
so small, she told herself. They are tiny. She started to tell
Harlan her idea about the odds, but maybe he hadn't
thought yet that someone might have grabbed Cindy, and
so she was quiet about it. She said, "I'm sure she'll be home
any minute."

They waited in the living room, hardly speaking. They
had different ways of waiting. Harlan sat, perched, on the
edge of a chair, or he walked back and forth, looking out
the front window, sometimes stepping onto the porch outside to look up and down the street. He paced, while June
sat on the couch where they had been just the night before
when everything seemed simple, or if not simple, at least
not horrifying. She put her hand on the seat of the couch

beside her. Cindy had talked about going to Mexico to find her father, but surely a ten-year-old wouldn't try to go that far away, and if she did try, someone would stop her. Little Babe jumped up on the couch and sat with her. If something bad had happened to Cindy, surely Little Babe would sense it, she told herself.

"She told me she wanted to see her father, in Mexico," June said.

"Her father?" Harlan repeated.

"She and Vernay talked about going there together." She hadn't planned on emphasizing this idea of Mexico, which seemed especially alarming, but she continued. "There's a book in her room, and it used to be opened to a page that told about a town with a name that sounded like *birthday*. It was a name like birthday in Spanish."

"You don't know anything about Vernay," he said. "You never even met her. Your big friend," he said. "You came here and fucked everything up, you know it? And for what?" He put his hand over his face, and June thought of that hand on her cheek, on her shoulder, under her hips lifting her up.

June thought suddenly of the kids' conversation in the lunch line about the Greyhound bus. *You don't even know what a Greyhound bus is,* someone had said. *Your mamma is too fat to fit on a Greyhound bus.* Who had said that?

"Can't we call the police?" Her voice was loud.

"I said no, didn't I?"

"But why not?" she shouted.

"What's gonna happen then? Nothing. Not a thing.

— *211* —

Nada." He corrected himself. "I'll tell you what will happen. What will happen is when I do find her, they'll send somebody to take her away. Don't you know anything?" He stood up and began to walk back and forth. "Why don't you just go home," he said, and in a voice that was almost kind, he added, "There's nothing you can do here."

"I don't want to go."

He hesitated and then said, "Okay, stay here. Fine. I'm going back to Mona's, and then I'll try the bus station again."

After he left, June stepped onto the front porch. She looked up and down the street. It was a Monday night, and most of the houses were dark.

Even if Cindy ran away, she'd be back. Kids start to run away, and then they don't. They stay out late, and then they get hungry, and they come home. June felt in her pocket for a cigarette, but she hadn't thought to bring them. Her car sat in front of the house, and she wondered if Cindy saw that car would she turn away and go someplace else, instead of home? How far could a ten-year-old get? She thought of the night before, when they had sat out here together. Surely a ten-year-old wouldn't hitchhike. June thought suddenly of a newspaper article she'd seen once, of a woman who had gone to Niagara Falls with her baby, and while she was there she had dropped that baby into the waterfall. She thought, Cindy is going over the waterfall and all we can do is stand helplessly by, watching.

She stood on the porch. When she had read that Niagara Falls story, she had thought the mother killed her child on purpose, but she didn't think that now. She thought, I'll find her, no matter where she is. She shut her eyes, and she saw the map of Mexico stretching from one ocean to the next. She thought of all the places between here and there, all the places a person could fit. Even if you considered only Oregon, or only this town, even if you only had to look in this neighborhood, there were too many places. And the idea of all those places filled her with desperation, and she thought suddenly of the movie they had watched, *The Premature Burial*. She thought of the man's body when they opened the coffin, his fingers bloody from clawing at the wood.

She began to walk back and forth on the porch. She had to rein herself in, if she was going to be any help at all. There were concrete things that could be addressed. Did Cindy have any money? That would make a difference. And where in Mexico did her father live? Had she left clues?

June went inside the house. She walked down the hall and opened Cindy's door. Had Harlan looked in here for clues, or had he panicked? She stood in the doorway looking in, and she thought of the police. The police had come here after Cindy's mother died, and they had dug around because when you're murdered your life is evidence. What did the police look for? Did they look through her clothes, in her drawers, in her closet? Did they ask about her boyfriends? Did they know about Bill?

She flipped the light switch and stepped into the room. Was there evidence about Cindy in here? *Just the facts, ma'am,* Joe Friday used to say, and it seemed like good advice. The first fact was the missing book. *Let's Go Mexico,* a book for college students. It had been Vernay's book. The first time June had come here, it had been lying open on the nightstand. When she cleaned the room, June had put it in a drawer, but it wasn't there now. Was that a clue or not? Would a ten-year-old runaway think to take a travel book with her? June looked around the room. Certainly she had more to go on than Sherlock Holmes ever did. He could notice that the cuffs of someone's sleeves were frayed and solve the mystery.

Cindy's bed was made, but it was rumpled, and that was because she had spent the day lying on it, crying, according to Harlan. Had Harlan said that, or had she imagined it? She opened Cindy's drawers, but they were still filled with clothes. Had Harlan watched her go? Had she carried anything with her? June looked in the closet at Cindy's shoes: red sneakers, a pair of cheap patent leather Mary Janes, rubber boots, sandals. A mother might be able to see what was missing, but June couldn't tell.

Cindy didn't have a mother, but she had other things. She had an uncle who loved her. She had Mona and Little Babe. She was a healthy child, and she was solid. She had something solid and substantial at her core, which you could sense about children sometimes. She had all those things. She had a sense of humor and a good memory. It's easy to think of ways that the kids are pitiful, but this is a disservice, June thought. She does not have bombs falling on her head. She has clean water to drink.

We live in a sweet old world, June thought, and it was a

song, the name of a song or lyrics in a song, but she couldn't remember any more than that. How hard would it be to get clean water to everyone in the world? she wondered. She picked up Cindy's pillow and held it to her face.

June went to the living room to wait. Any minute Harlan was sure to come home with Cindy. They were undoubtedly on their way back right now, and Harlan was so relieved that he wasn't even mad.

June heard a car, and before she even got to the front door, it flew open and Mona burst into the house. "What do you think you're doing here?" she shouted.

"You haven't seen Cindy?" June asked, and she went to the door to look out. "She's not with you?"

Mona grabbed her arm and pulled June around to face her. June thought the other woman would hit her, but she only shoved her backward and cried, "Who do you think you are coming here like this? You didn't even know Vernay. You never even met her. We had a good thing before you came along." She pointed her finger at June. "If anything happens to that girl, you'll be sorry. You hear me?"

But then Mona turned suddenly, to look out the door behind her. She lowered her voice. "We got the cops coming and going all of a sudden." She tilted her chin to a police car that had turned onto the street and was headed their way. "Just act regular, now. Don't look at him."

When the car had driven on by, Mona pulled the door shut. She went to the window and looked out, and then she turned back to June. "That Bill," she said, "your *husband*, I met him, nice-looking and all, snappy dresser, and I says to myself, 'Don't you trust a man who irons his blue jeans.' I says to myself, 'If something looks too good to be true, you can bet it is.' " She paused and then added, "Whatever kind of thing the two of you have got going here, I'll figure it out."

"Did you see Harlan? Did he find you?"

Mona frowned and shook her head. "She was going to hitchhike and she would've done it too. You know how she is—just like her mother—stubborn and willful—and would he have been happy then? You can't let a ten-year-old hitch-hike."

"You gave her a ride?" June grabbed the other woman's arm. "Is that what happened?"

But Mona would not be rushed. "I said to myself, 'Well, if I don't help, no telling what could happen. She could end up like her mother.' " She looked at June quizzically. "What would be the odds such a thing could happen to a mother, and then to her daughter too? So, I took her to Portland, to her granny's house, that's all. You'd think I committed mur-der from the way Harlan acted."

"That's where she is? At her granny's house?" June took a deep breath. All this time she was just at her grandma's. June thought of her own grandmother, with her warm house and something always cooking on the stove.

Mona went to the window and peered out the Venetian blinds. "Somebody ought to call about that poor fucking dog they got tied up over there, barks day and night, and nobody pays attention to it. One day that man over there— I saw him poke his head out and yell, 'If you don't shut the fuck up, I'm going to cut your head off!' Yells it at his own dog, can you believe that? The world is full of nuts, I'm telling you." And then she turned back to June.

"I drove her all the way up there, to Portland. I had to borrow gas money from my brother, Sam. I had to get ten bucks from him, and even then I barely made it back. And after all that, Harlan goes and throws a hissy fit."

"I'm sure he was just worried."

"The old lady is her granny. I don't care what problem Harlan's got with her, she's still flesh and blood."

"It sounds like you did the right thing."

"The last thing I said to her was, call your uncle."

"What a relief," June said.

"What are you so worried about? It's none of your business. You don't even know these people. You never even met Vernay. I couldn't believe it when I heard that. You never even met her. You come here and take her clothes—I said to Harlan, I said we ought to call the cops on this, but Harlan said no. I said maybe next time we get a news reporter coming around, we could sell him the story. People like to read about things like this, sick things, and they'll pay money—"

But June wasn't going to talk about this now.

"Has he gone to get her?" she asked.

Mona didn't like being interrupted, and she snapped, "He's gone to find her, yeah. He's on his way to Portland right now."

"What do you mean, he's on his way to find her? You told me she's at her grandma's!"

"I said I took her to her granny's house. That's what I

said." Mona said the words carefully, as if she'd already spoken them, and June had been too slow-witted to understand.

She took Cindy to her granny's house in Portland, doing them all a big favor, she said, but when Harlan found that out, he threw a fit. A shitfit, she called it this time. He phoned the grandmother's house, but Cindy had left, and so Harlan was on his way up there, to look for her. Who knows where she could have gone?

"The grandmother let her leave?"

"The whole family's crazy, I'm telling you."

The women had moved into the living room, and now June sat down on the couch. "There's got to be some logical explanation," she said. It occurred to her that she kept using this phrase, *logical explanation.*

"Do you have a cigarette?" she asked.

"I quit four days ago," said Mona, but she began to look around. She went to the kitchen, and June could hear her opening drawers. She could hear her, finally, in the refrigerator. When she came back, Mona had a bowl of ice cream.

She sat down across from June, and she said, "I ran away from home myself when I was a girl. That's after my father left and my mother, she took up with this guy name of Red, a redheaded man, and he had a little boy, the sweetest thing, but I'd hate to see him now, after getting raised by his daddy. Now my kids, they're with their dad, but he's never laid a hand on anybody, got himself a farm, the kind with milk cows, that's where he works, and they live there too. So it's nice, kids living on a farm with cows and all, even if it wasn't exactly my cup of tea." Mona paused and then added, "My mama never had any sense about men, some women are just like that, same as Vernay, no sense about men at all."

June could hear the clock on the wall. Almost midnight. Harlan would be near Woodburn by now. He would be in Portland in less than an hour, and then he would call, surely, and tell them what he had found. The grandmother must know where Cindy is, June told herself.

"He won't find her," Mona predicted.

"Then we ought to go to Portland ourselves," June said, "if we don't know anything by morning. We could start at the grandma's house—"

Mona looked at her sideways. "What's it to you?" she asked. "Harlan, he wants to make excuses for you, but I said to him, I said, 'I bet this lady is writing a crime book, you know like at the supermarket, true crime, and she's going to make a million bucks on Vernay,' and now, hey, if anything happens to Cindy, then it looks like you hit the jackpot, doesn't it?" She set down her bowl of ice cream.

"I'm not writing any fucking book!"

"Don't you cuss me!"

"He meant to kill me and not her, that's the point. He was after me."

Mona faltered. "What are you talking about?"

"He went to my house, he knew where I lived, and he went to wait for me, but Vernay was there instead."

Mona went to a table in the corner and jerked open a

drawer. She dug around until she found an old pack of Camels, and there was one cigarette in it. She put it in her mouth and lit it, and then she sat back down across from June, and June told the story again, more slowly.

First she told the story of her car. She told about Ralphie Pruett's father stopping to help. She told about the woman in the red coat coming out of her house on Jackson Street and looking at both of them. Whether it was a red coat or not didn't matter anymore, and she didn't worry about it. She told about opening the paper later and seeing his picture, and about Cindy at school. She told about stopping by the house, to see where Cindy lived. She told about one thing leading to another.

Mona listened without interrupting. She looked philosophical. And then, finally, she said, "Funny, isn't it, that you might wind up getting them both killed?"

Chapter 26

They waited up until the middle of the night, but Cindy didn't come back and Harlan didn't call, and so finally they tried to sleep. Mona went to lie down in Harlan's bed but June chose the couch.

She lay down and shut her eyes. It was here that Harlan had found her only the night before. Sex is not worth it, she thought. As good as it can be, it isn't worth all the trouble it brings.

She was not going to think of what might happen to Cindy. She was going to sleep, or at least shut her eyes and think of nothing, and in the morning, they would go to Portland, to the grandmother's house. June couldn't understand why some men liked to hurt children.

The grandmother lived in a little apartment off Sandy Boulevard in Portland. A sign across the front of the building said *Del Mar Apartments* in italics. It had never been a fancy place, but still it must have seen better days than these. The paint was peeling, and the front steps were cracked. The small yard was full of weeds and patches of bare dirt. There were eighteen apartments in all, six going across and three up. They each had a balcony, but when someone hears the word *balcony,* they might think of lawn chairs and flowers, and that would be a mistake here at the Del Mar. The balconies were empty, or they were full of boxes and garbage bags, and some of the windows were cracked. American flags flew from three windows, June observed, so we would make no mistake regarding what country we were in.

"If you could live anywhere, where would it be?" she had asked Cindy, and Cindy, who had a twenty-second rule about questions like this, had quickly replied, "America is the best!" but then she added, "Mexico, I think."

June had her hands on her hips, looking at the building, and now she wiped them on her pants. Mona was quiet for once.

"Which one is hers?" June asked.

But Mona didn't answer. She went to the front door. It was unlocked and she stepped inside, with June and Little Babe following. They were in a small entryway with mailboxes off to one side. Mona stopped to read the names written on them.

"Don't you know which one it is?" asked June.

Mona ran her fingers over the names. "There's no Hanks here," Mona said. "Can you see a Hanks?"

But June ignored her question. She stood back, looking

around her. The doorway led to a staircase or down a long hallway. The building was dark, as if the bulbs had gone out and nobody thought to replace them, and the paint was old and dirty. The floor was covered with a cheap carpet that was stained and torn, and it smelled like someone used the wall as a urinal.

"Look, June. This is it, ennit?" Mona pointed to one of the names. "Apartment two-oh-four."

During their two-hour drive to Portland, June had regretted bringing Mona, who had spent that time recounting the details of every grisly crime she could think of, but now June was glad to have someone else along. They climbed the stairs and knocked on the door to Apartment 204. It was a blue door, an unlucky door, and they could hear someone on the other side of it. They waited.

"Jeez, I need a cigarette," said Mona, and she stepped forward, knocking again. She had looked nervous, but now she was irritated. Mona wore a T-shirt and shorts. She wore red flip-flops. She had not dressed up for the city, no. She had her orange hair pulled away from her face. Her skin was bad, but she was lovely, really, and her presence at that moment, against all reason, made June feel safe, although June did hope she wouldn't talk too much or say the wrong thing, whatever that was.

Cindy's grandmother was a large woman in a sleeveless housedress. She had fat white arms, short blonde frizzy hair, and small blue eyes. She had tiny feet. She stood in the doorway, barring their way. She looked too robust to be somebody's grandma.

"I have no idea where she went. I have no idea at all."
The woman leaned out of the doorway and looked up and
down the hall. "Are you social workers?"

June explained that they were friends. They had come
to see if they could find Cindy. They wondered if they
could just step inside and talk.

But the grandmother crossed her arms. She said, "I
already been through all this with Harlan. He stood right
where you are now, and I told him, I have no idea where she
went to. She snuck off." The grandmother had tiny white
teeth and pink lips. She said, "I hoped his temper had got
better, but he is the same as always. He is just like his father."

"He doesn't have a temper," said Mona.

"It's going to get him in trouble one of these days," the
older woman continued.

She was barring their way, but Mona pushed on
through, into the apartment, making a path, which June
followed. "You can't bring that dog in here," she called
after them, but Mona only stooped to pick Little Babe up.

The women showed themselves into the living room
where they sat side by side on the couch. The television was
on. "You hold that dog then," the woman said. "Hold it on
your lap." A chair stood across from them, but instead of
sitting in it, Mrs. Hanks stood behind it with her hands on
its back. She was dressed in a sleeveless housedress, but she
was sweating.

"Don't let it down," she told Mona, referring, again, to
Little Babe.

A game show was on the television, and someone had

just won. She jumped up and down like a cheerleader, which is what they have to agree to do, June had heard, in order to be on TV. They had to agree to jump up and down and make fools of themselves, but you can't blame them. A paperback novel sat on the table beside the chair, with a cup of coffee next to it.

June moved a small, round pillow from the couch in back of her and held it on her lap. She told Mrs. Hanks that they were only trying to help. They wondered if she might have some idea where Cindy could have gone. She didn't like the other woman, but she spoke kindly. She was grateful that Mona kept quiet. She leaned forward, looking up into the older woman's face, smiling, asking who else Cindy knew. Who in Portland? An old friend or neighbor? June suggested. Or maybe there were cousins? She spoke in a loud voice, in order to be heard over the television.

"They don't have any family here," said Mona, but June didn't look at her.

"Could she be in one of the other apartments? Maybe someone has a kid—"

"Nobody here has kids! Some have got dogs, and they bark all the time. We've got a noise clause in our contracts, but they let their dogs bark."

June had told herself to pay attention to all things. There are clues everywhere, at least according to detective shows on TV. There are clues in the way the curtains are pulled shut, in the plastic covering the lamp, clues in the hems of people's clothes, in their fingernails, everywhere there are signs and clues. She looked at the woman's hands holding onto the chair, rings on three fingers and the nails neat and trimmed, polished pink.

The room was dark, and June wanted to turn on a light or throw the curtains open. She got up and turned off the television and for a moment silence engulfed them.

"She isn't but ten years—" Mona began, but Mrs. Hanks interrupted.

"That's just what I thought. She's ten years old, where does she think she's going?"

"Could she have gone to the Greyhound station?" asked June.

"Did you know Vernay?" the older woman asked. "Were you friends with her?"

"I was," said Mona. "I knew her real good, but this lady here"—she indicated June—"never even met her."

"I still can't believe what happened. I'll never get over it, I tell you. How can you get over something like that?"

"You can't," said Mona. "I know when my dad died, I never did get over it. He weighed over four hundred pounds—"

"They sent a cop to tell me what happened to her. He was young-looking, looked like a Boy Scout. They sent him here to tell me, and I took it hard. Despite everything, she was my little girl." Mrs. Hanks came around in front of the chair and sat down. "You got to love them no matter what. They are your own flesh and blood, and you love them. You don't have a choice. It's human nature." She looked at June. "Do you have children?"

"She's a teacher," said Mona, quickly. "She was Cindy's teacher."

"When he told me what happened to her, I had to sit down. I sat down right here." Mrs. Hanks indicated the chair she was sitting on.

Suddenly she reached down and pulled out a photo album. She opened the pages and handed the book to the women. There was a picture of a baby, lying on a couch. A picture of a toddler and a little boy in front of a tiny Christmas tree. A girl holding a puppy. There was a large school photograph of a girl who was clearly Vernay. She looked about fourteen: a pretty girl with chestnut-colored hair and big brown eyes.

Maybe they were supposed to stop now and help Mrs. Hanks process the murder of her daughter, but June didn't want to. "We're looking for Cindy," she reminded her.

"She came here and said she was looking for her father, *a Mexican,* she said."

"What did you tell her?"

"He is not Mexican. I don't know where she came up with that. He is American. He is a dark-haired American gentleman, a Christian, from my church." She pointed to a photograph of a little girl wearing a cowboy hat. "I couldn't believe it when Harlan told me he had gone and had her cremated. He didn't even wait to let me see her. I'm still her mother, whether he likes it or not. I'm her mother."

There were hardly any pictures of Harlan in the album.

"What he doesn't know," she continued, "is that somebody's got to be at the funeral home, watching, or they'll just throw the bodies out anywhere they want and then tell you they were cremated. They give you some phony ashes and say, 'This here is your loved one.' If you watch the news, you know these things. They put the dead bodies in the woods and then save the money."

"I never heard of such a thing," said June.

"Well, then you don't watch the news, do you?"

"I saw it," said Mona. "They found all those bodies out in the woods in Michigan or someplace."

"I'm sure that didn't happen here," said June quickly.

"That's what everybody tells themselves," said Mrs. Hanks. A small yellow cat ran through the room, hiding under the chair where the woman sat. "You hold that dog!" she exclaimed, but Little Babe wasn't interested in cats. "See there, I told you not to bring a dog. She doesn't like dogs." The woman bent forward, wiggling her fingers under the chair.

"Where is her father now? Do you know?" asked June.

"I guess they told you all those things about him, and you believed it."

Mona started to answer, "We don't know—" but June interrupted.

"We don't know what to believe." June was in a hurry. She wanted to stand up and run through the apartment, throw open every door, dig through every cupboard, turn the whole place upside down. She wanted to open the window and scream Cindy's name, but sometimes, she knew, in order to go fast, we must slow down. When Mrs. Hanks didn't respond, June asked, "Where would she go to look for her father?"

"Her father doesn't have anything to do with this," said Mrs. Hanks quickly.

"Cindy said she thought he was in Mexico," June insisted.

"We're not even sure who the father was."

"What do you mean you're not sure?" asked Mona. "You said he was from your church."

"I don't know what Vernay tells people," Mrs. Hanks said, and then she added, "It could have been anybody." She pulled the hem of her housedress over her knees.

"Anybody?" Mona was angry. "It could have been anybody? She was in high school."

"It's easy for girls to say things. They can say anything, and how's a man going to defend himself? He can't! She can say anything she wants, anything at all. And Harlan"—she pointed at June—"if it wasn't for him, everything would have been fine."

"Harlan?" June asked. She would not believe anything this woman said. She would not believe it. But Mrs. Hanks had said the man went to her church. He was a black-haired Christian from her church. It was like the guessing game, Twenty Questions, and she had played the way some of the younger children played—guessing randomly, wildly, instead of starting out with big categories and narrowing things down.

"There is nothing more selfish or jealous than children. They don't care if you're happy or not."

It was dawning on June. She should have guessed right away. She worked in a school. She knew what happened to girls sometimes. She had heard the rumor too: incest in the family. "Cindy's father was your boyfriend, wasn't he?"

Mona gasped. "Her boyfriend!"

Mrs. Hanks stood up. "He's not here now, is he? Do you see him? He's gone. He was going to adopt Vernay, did she tell you that part? She always leaves that part out. She forgets to mention all the things he bought for her or how nice he was. He could be real nice. Ask anybody. Everyone loved him. We were engaged, and he was going to give her his name and everything."

"Does Cindy know about him?" asked June.

"It was a long time ago now. How many years? Eleven years ago and here I sit. But, like I told Cindy, it's water over the dam, that's what I said."

"You told her? You told Cindy?"

June's voice was quiet, but Mona took up the question now, shouting, "Is that what happened? Is that why she ran away?"

Mona jumped up and stood over the woman. "You told her—" she shouted, but June stood up too now and took her arm.

"Let's get out of here. Come on." Mona hesitated, and June added, "She can't help us. She doesn't know anything." June put her hand on Mona's back. There is a place on the back, the same place we pat when we are holding babies, and June put her hand there and pressed. "Let's just go."

Chapter 27

They sat in June's car outside the grandmother's apartment building. June didn't know where to go next, and she fought a rising panic. She gripped the steering wheel, but she didn't start the car.

"No wonder Harlan about had a heart attack when I said I brought her here," said Mona. "Bitch."

They could hear a baby crying. It was a noisy street. There were cars and buses. Two old men sat at a bus stop arguing. A muscular man in a tight black shirt stood on the corner. June didn't want to think of Cindy here. At school she was one of the big kids, but she wasn't big at all. She was little.

This very minute something terrible could be happening to her, June thought, and if we could just go to the right place, if we could open the right door, we could stop it. We could bring her home. And she wanted to throw open every door in the city and search each room, until they found her.

"Did I tell you about that black girl who got killed here

last summer? She had a job working at Wendy's, you know, the hamburger place. She walked there every day, sixteen blocks from her house, saving money for college. She was going to go to the community college. And then one day a lawyer's office finds her outside in the bushes, but they'd turned the sprinkler on, you know how dry it was, and they'd washed away the evidence." Mona looked over at June. "Want me to drive?"

June looked down at her hands on the steering wheel. She thought suddenly of an old abandoned car she and her cousins used to play in when they were kids. It was an emerald green car, and it had a shiny, thick steering wheel, and in the center of it there was a red stone, which they thought was a ruby. They'd sit all day in that car.

Mona said, "And when she was out of college, that girl was going to get a good job and help all her brothers and sisters. There were nine kids in that family, did I tell you that part?"

But June didn't answer. "I guess we don't have to worry about Mexico anymore," she said.

"I guess not."

"Do they have other family?" June asked. "What about Harlan and Vernay's father?"

"He was out of the picture."

"There must be someone else, cousins or someone."

"I think they got people out in Kansas, but she wouldn't've known any of them," said Mona, and then added, "When I think of what could be happening to her this very minute." She looked over at June. "Let me drive," she said. "You look terrible."

Mona said they should look first at Pioneer Courthouse Square because that was where the runaways go. She said next they should try to find out where Vernay and Cindy had lived when they lived in Portland, and go to that neighborhood. Along with these ideas, Mona interspersed many observations and details. They drove toward downtown, and Mona talked. June thought if Mona's words were text, she would read them with a yellow highlighter, marking out the main points, and they would be Pioneer Square and Cindy's old neighborhood. Her next thought was to place her hand over Mona's mouth.

They drove along Sandy Boulevard, and Mona said, "Eighty-second and Sandy is where the whores go, but we won't find her there."

"Of course we won't find her there, Mona! For crying out loud!"

But Mona was the expert, and she said, "Lots of runaways end up whores."

June rolled her window down. It was late morning, and she had forgotten to call the school. She leaned her head against the seat and shut her eyes. She'd never go back there again. She suddenly knew it. She would be like the kids, one day simply gone, with no good-byes, no exchange of addresses, no farewell cupcakes, nothing, no closure as they called it. She was different than she had been before all this business. She had always been steady and calm. She had worried and obsessed about things, but she had always moved forward.

She thought it must be nice to be Catholic and go to confession and start again. She had been Catholic as a child, but a child couldn't appreciate an opportunity like this.

They passed apartment buildings and strip clubs. They passed convenience stores, Laundromats, and hotels that advertised hourly rates. They passed a tall black man in a leather miniskirt and high heels, and Mona said, "There goes somebody's son."

"I'd feel a lot better if we could call the cops," said June.

The signs called Portland "the City of Roses." It was too early for roses, but flowers bloomed in people's yards and, as they got closer to the inner city, crabapples and cherry trees bloomed along the streets. It was a beautiful city, a city of flowers.

Mona said they would go to Pioneer Courthouse Square and ask around. She had a picture of Cindy in her wallet, and they would show it to the kids there. And then, she said, they'd find a phone so June could call Bill and ask if he knew the neighborhood where Vernay and Cindy used to live.

"He won't know that," said June quickly.

June thought of Cindy's father. She had imagined Cindy's father in Mexico, with a big Mexican family. She had imagined a grandmother and aunts, uncles, cousins, the more the merrier, every child a blessing, but instead there was this other man.

They parked downtown and walked to the square. The area was surrounded on two sides by brick stairs that led down to a large plaza. On one edge of the plaza was a fountain. There was a cart that sold giant burritos. All around stood tall buildings with shiny, clean windows: stores and offices, a bank, restaurants.

Businesspeople walked through the plaza with attaché cases, in expensive suits or dresses, with polished leather shoes. It had stopped raining, and people carried their umbrellas folded up. Students sat in the square, reading books. An elderly man in a plaid kilt and running shoes played a guitar. Homeless people sat in the plaza. Two men slept. Another read a thick paperback. Kids hung out, talking in loud voices; some had tattoos and orange or blue hair, others wore leather clothes or torn blue jeans—hair in spikes or no hair at all. Some of the kids had dogs, and one girl held a kitten.

Mona approached a group playing Hacky Sack. She held out the picture of Cindy for them to see. They shook their heads. They hadn't seen Cindy, they said. No. "She's awful young," said the girl with the kitten. "She's just a little kid."

June and Mona sat down on a bench and watched the passersby.

"I've got two boys myself," said Mona, "about the same age of these kids here." She nodded to the kids playing Hacky Sack. "They're back in Wisconsin with their dad."

It started to rain softly, but the kids kept playing their game, the man kept playing his guitar, the people kept doing what they were doing. It was a light rain and if people had umbrellas, they didn't open them.

"They're on a farm near Lake Mills. You heard of it?"

"No."

"They got pyramids there, from the Indians. Not big pyramids like what you get in Egypt, but they're still pyramids. We used to go out there at night and walk around. You can walk right over them. We were out there one night, this was years back, and I was lying on the ground. It gets cold in Wisconsin, let me tell you, brother, it gets fucking cold. So we were there one summer night, my husband and me, and he's sitting in the car, drinking a beer, but I'm laying out under the stars. I'm there, and he's in the car, and I can hear him calling me. 'Mona, come on,' he's yelling. And I think it will always be like this for me and him. Me lying under the stars on pyramids, and him sitting in the car with a bottle of beer. That's when I knew I was out of there."

Mona didn't seem like the kind of woman who would lie beneath the stars, thought June, but what do we know about anyone else?

"He's a good dad, lives on the farm, plays baseball. He's a big Packers fan, course, and so are the boys." She hesitated, adding, "I guess I'll go back there someday, to be close to my boys again."

"To Wisconsin?"

"I'd go to Milwaukee."

A girl Cindy's size walked by, and both women turned to watch her, but it wasn't Cindy.

"We'll never find her this way," said June.

"You got a better idea?" But then Mona rubbed her arms. "We ought to get something to eat while we're down here." The skin of her legs was pale and smooth, and she jiggled her foot up and down. This was not the time to give up cigarettes, she said, more than once. She thought maybe she'd get one from one of the kids. They all smoked. How they paid for it, who knows, she said.

It had stopped drizzling and, for a moment, the sun came out.

"I wonder why he didn't grab you when he had a chance," said Mona.

"I told you that woman came out of her house just then."

"The woman in the red coat."

Was it red or not? June didn't know.

She said, "I stood next to him, Mona, and I didn't feel anything. Shouldn't you feel danger?" She used to think she knew about people, but she didn't. Her whole life with Bill was a lie that she had let herself believe. She thought, Right now I want to begin again. I want to be honest, and I want to look at people and see what's there, and know if that coat is red or not.

"Don't you think it's funny," said Mona, "that this Pruett guy was going to kill you, Bill's wife, and instead he winds up killing Vernay, Bill's girlfriend? I've been trying to figure out what connects the two of you. You both look the same, that's one thing. Got the same hair and figure and all." She was quiet, and then she added, "Sometimes they look for a woman like their mother."

"Pruett told the cops he went to my house to wait for me, and that's how he found her. He says he's innocent—"

"They all say that."

"He told them he'd been following me for a while, and he went to my house, but Vernay was there."

But Mona wasn't listening to her now. "Maybe it's your Bill who goes for the same type."

The waitress at McMurray's was blonde, but June didn't mention that. "He admitted giving her a ride."

"He couldn't get around that," Mona countered. "Everybody saw her in the car with him." And then she added, "She always was unlucky."

June stood up and walked back and forth in front of the bench where Mona sat. "She had a fight with Bill, and she came over when she knew I'd be getting home."

"That sounds like Vernay."

They'd had a fight, Bill said, because he had broken off with her. She wouldn't leave, and then he'd pushed her out, and she'd fallen on their stairs. He only wanted to be with June, he said, he knew that now, but even if it was true, it was too late.

The women sat watching the kids who had run away from their homes, who played Hacky Sack and smoked cigarettes, talked too loud, laughed, and sometimes sang or danced. They were grown-up versions of Missy and Mikey Black, but they probably weren't fire-starters because those children get locked away. June thought of Mikey and wondered where he was. He'd like it here, she thought, but Pioneer Courthouse Square was out of reach for someone like him.

She thought, Even the Green River Killer was a child

once. What happens? But she knew what happens. When you don't work with kids, but only read about them in the paper, you think, why didn't somebody do something?

She would never go back to the school again. Once she had thought she made a difference, but now she didn't. June had gotten too personal with the kids and too personal with her job and too wrapped up and personal about everything. She couldn't draw the proper lines around things anymore. She'd get a job at a restaurant, she thought. There would be no insurance, but at least you don't get involved with everyone. At a restaurant when someone has a big problem it's because they don't like their dinner, and your biggest hardship is being cheerful all the time.

"Stress makes me hungry," said Mona. "Does it make you hungry?"

"No."

"I just quit smoking. I need to eat." When June didn't respond, she added, "If we go to a restaurant, there'll be a phone."

There was a little Mexican restaurant not far from the square, and the women walked there and went inside. There were purple and green piñatas hanging from the ceiling. There were signs that said, "Fiesta!" A man with bad teeth took their order, tacos and enchiladas, while a woman stood at a steam table and cooked. She had her hair in a black bun and a crucifix around her neck. It was still early for dinner, but people began to come in. Two young kids came in and sat at a table close to the kitchen, doing schoolwork. A couple sat at a booth next to Mona and June. An old man came in. He stopped to talk to the couple. He looked at the children's homework.

There was a phone in the corner, and the women got change and made their phone calls. The Hankses' number was busy, so June dialed her own number and waited.

He answered right away. "June!" His voice was loud and worried. "Where the hell are you? I finally went to Vernay's and the only person there was that brother of Mona's." Mona's brother was waiting at the house in case Cindy came home, but June didn't explain that to Bill. Bill didn't know what had gotten into June. She used to be so reasonable. What was she thinking? He said Cindy was just fooling around. "She'll be back as soon as she gets hungry."

June listened with her eyes shut. She imagined him in their kitchen beneath the rack of hanging pots. Whenever she imagined Bill, he was always in the kitchen or in their bedroom, and it was always warm. They didn't own their house, but they had lived in it for six years, and they were wholehearted renters. They had made it their home. They had painted the walls, and she had planted flowers. She had planted roses because they were Bill's favorite flower, and she had put in honeysuckle outside their bedroom window so that in summer their room was filled with its sweet smell. They had planted blueberries and raspberries. Once an eagle had landed in a tree in their yard.

"When will you be back?" he asked. "I'll come and get you right now. I'll leave this minute."

They had met at a restaurant. She had turned in an

order one night, and he had been there to take it. It was a seafood restaurant, down by the water. My name is Bill, he'd said. He had looked at her. It was a Saturday night, and it was going to be busy. When she said her name, he had said, "Flaming June, like the painting."

She knew the painting he meant. It was a woman lying back in an orange dress, with dark hair spread out on her arm. She did look like the woman in the painting. She had always secretly thought so.

From that first moment, he had seen things in her that only she had known about herself, but now she wondered if this was the way he was with all women.

"I was thinking maybe we ought to try her old neighborhood," June said. She hesitated. "Do you know where they used to live, Cindy and her mom, when they were up here?"

This was a sore point, and he paused. "The Hawthorne area," he said.

How long had he known her? She wanted to ask, but she didn't want to know. It felt nicer when she was thinking of Flaming June. He had bought her a print of that painting. It was her favorite colors, orange and yellow.

Someone had told her once that love is limitless, but that couldn't be right, she thought.

"Do you mean on Hawthorne Street?"

"I don't know where she lived, June. Jesus. I only met her last year."

She didn't want to know about when they met, but she heard herself ask, "One year exactly?"

"I said one year."

"You mean last May? Or last summer?" If it was May, then she would have been at work.

"What does it matter?"

She didn't want it to be May, when she was at work and the honeysuckle bloomed, but she didn't tell him that. "Hawthorne is a big neighborhood," she said.

"It's on Twenty-third, two blocks off Hawthorne. It's a big pink house—the landlord actually let her paint it pink, if you can believe that. Not that I ever saw the house," he added quickly, "but she told me about it."

It wasn't true that love was limitless, she thought. Love was finite. You only had so much, and then it was gone.

"It's across the street from an old man who does upholstery." That seemed like a lot to know about someone. "I don't know how you think you're going to find her, June."

"We tried the grandmother."

"I could have told you that would be futile."

"Don't you know a lot!"

He didn't argue with her. He said he was supposed to leave for work, but he could call in. "We could spend the evening together," he said. "Baby, I am so sorry." And then, because he could never leave good enough alone, he added, "But you know she didn't mean anything."

He waited for her to answer, and then he said, "I'll make you something to eat."

"I'm at a restaurant right now."

The door opened, and June turned to see a family come in. A man with a cowboy hat and a woman walking beside him with a baby on her hip. The man took his hat off, and June turned back to face the wall.

"You know you aren't perfect either," Bill said.

She could hear the woman talking to the baby. She had a sweet voice and June strained to hear the words, but she couldn't. She thought of Cindy sitting on her grandmother's couch, hearing who her real father was. She thought of Vernay, the girl with hair like her hair, the girl who wanted to be a deer, who wanted to live in a hot place, who fell in love with Bill. She thought of Bill, her husband, and she wondered, Was it all a waste? That's what people say sometimes, I wasted ten years of my life. I wasted the best years.

On the other end, he was talking. His voice was low and urgent. *Baby,* he called her. It seemed like her life with Bill was a deck of cards spread out on a table—hearts, spades, diamonds, and clubs. They were all there. She thought that for some people things must be like a deck of cards with only the top one showing.

She turned to watch the mother. She wondered if Bill only saw the top card or if he was like her, but she didn't know. You'd think you'd know this about someone after ten years, she thought.

The woman saw her staring, and June shifted her eyes to Mona, who waved and pointed to their table. The food was ready.

"Just go to work, Bill," she said, and she hung up the phone.

"What'd he say?" Mona asked when she had sat down at the table.

June took a bite of her dinner. When she had swallowed it, she wiped her mouth, and answered. "Twenty-third Street, two blocks off Hawthorne." And then she added, "He says I'm not perfect either."

"That son of a bitch."

But June didn't want to think about him anymore. She should mention that the house was pink, but she didn't want to. She wanted to sit and eat her enchiladas and listen to the voice of the woman talking to her baby and the sound of the children doing their schoolwork.

Mona said, "I told Vernay, I told her, he's married, but she wouldn't believe it. She didn't want to believe it. People believe what they want."

"He's a good liar," said June, and it wasn't like she was talking about Bill at all, but like she was reading a script, a script called *cheating husband.* She read along, and other people read along, and even her thoughts read along.

She thought of Bill, Bill at home, Bill in the car, Bill at work, Bill in his chef's hat, Bill at the beach, Bill, Bill, Bill, and it had nothing to do with this other Bill, the cheating husband Bill.

From the window she could see the sidewalk. People walked by in expensive clothes, clothes that looked like they had never been worn before. Bill would say they all have their problems, but June couldn't sympathize with them. And anyway, what Bill said didn't count anymore. He had given up his right to count. She thought of what the principal had said about the hot burning coal of resentment, drop that coal. But she didn't want to drop it.

"I'd hate to be the man who harmed a hair on the head of that little girl," said Mona. "Harlan will kill him."

"Okay, let's think about this," said June. "She left her grandmother's house—and then what? She took the bus, let's say. She lived here before and she would have known how to take a bus, right? Did she know how to take a bus?"

Mona shrugged. "Sure."

"She'd go someplace she knew, wouldn't she? Wouldn't she go back to where she lived with Vernay? She'd have friends near there. Or she'd have friends from school. What school did she go to?"

Mona shook her head.

June got an ink pen from her purse. She wrote on a napkin: *Hawthorne neighborhood, friend from school.* "We need to be systematic," she said. She wrote *Kansas.*

"She wouldn't go to Kansas," said Mona.

"Let's include everything we can think of."

"Hitchhike," suggested Mona.

June started to point out that it was a list of places, not means of transportation, but she didn't. *Hitchhike,* she wrote.

"The police have special departments designed to figure this stuff out," June said.

"They're not going to waste their time on people like us."

"Then we'll have to hire a private detective."

"You've watched too many movies."

June looked at her list. First they'd go to Twenty-third Street and knock on every door. She was not going to think about it too much. She was not going to think of what might happen to Cindy. She was going to figure out what needed to be done and do it.

"At least we know she'd put up a fight," said Mona optimistically. "They found that little girl who got killed over in Junction City, and she had the man's skin under her fingernails where she'd clawed him. That'd be our Cindy."

But this was too much, and June lowered her head and put her hands over her face. She pressed her eyes. She picked up a napkin to wipe her face but saw the list of places written on it and began to cry.

Mona stood up, went around the table to where June sat, and squatted next to her. "Hey! Hey! No. Shhh. It's okay. It's all right. You'll see. It's going to be just fine." June looked up. The man behind the counter started to come forward, but June shook her head. Mona handed her a glass of water and she took a drink.

Mona said, "I'm going to call Harlan's. I bet Sam knows something by now. You'll see. Harlan must have called with news by now—good news, I bet. You wait and see."

June watched Mona as she stood at the phone. She had been calm when she called Bill, but now her heart raced. She leaned forward watching Mona's back. Everything could hinge on this one phone call. She felt like she was in an emergency room, waiting to hear news, and now the doctor was walking toward her. She held her breath. June wished Mona would turn around so she could see her face. She wanted to stand close to Mona so she could hear what was being said, but she couldn't move. Everyone here was happy. They ate and smiled, they talked in quiet voices, they laughed. She was not going to think of what might be happening. She was not going to think of the little girl in Junction City. She was not going to think of Cindy jumping rope, Cindy in the lunch line, Cindy with Little Babe. She wasn't going to think of any of it. And then finally Mona began to turn. She began to turn around. Even before she spoke June was flooded with relief.

"She's fine! She's fine!" Mona shouted across the restaurant.

June didn't remember getting up, but she found herself at Mona's side. Two words and the world shifted. She was fine. She was just fine.

"She's on her way home!" exclaimed Mona. "She's with Harlan, on her way home." June felt like she had just won a million dollars. She felt like the woman on the game show back in Mrs. Hanks' house. Any minute she might jump up and down and kiss everyone in the room.

Mona was talking into the phone, but she stopped long enough to say, "What'd I tell you?" And then she was quiet again, listening.

"She was back in their old neighborhood. What'd I tell you?" said Mona. "She went back there and stayed with a friend there—if the mother had half a brain, she would have wondered about it—and that's where Harlan found her, at the neighbor's house. All along!" Mona held the phone to her ear, but she talked to June. "She should be whipped for this, you know, scaring everybody half to death, he should take a belt to her, but he won't." She said these things, but she smiled.

"Where are they?" June asked, but Mona was listening to her brother on the other end now, and waved her away. June was too excited to sit down. She walked to their table and back again. She got the tab and paid it, watching Mona, smiling at everyone.

"Someone was missing, but now she's found," she explained to the man behind the counter as he took her money. "A little girl!" she exclaimed and everyone in the room smiled at her. She turned to look at the room. "Fiesta!" the signs read, and they no longer seemed out of place.

Chapter 28

A ll that worrying for nothing, Bill would say, but June
was superstitious; she thought of worrying as a vacci-
nation against calamity. She and Bill were so different. How
had she ever imagined that they were perfect for each
other?

They drove home on the interstate, and Mona talked.
Mona said that down in California, if you pass a car at night
and they don't have their lights on, don't blink to remind
them, because it's a gang initiation, and they'll kill you.
Mona said if a cop tries to pull you over, you don't have to
stop if you're a woman, because how do you know it's a
real cop. Mona said if someone in a parking lot comes up
and wants to spray your wrist with a free sample of perfume, tell them no, because it's a trick. Mona said if June
was going to live on her own, she had to know these things.

June had lived with Bill for ten years. She knew there
were things she needed to know now, but they weren't
things like don't blink your lights. She would miss him. Was

it all right to realize that, or did she have to present a united front to herself? She'd move here, to the city, she thought, away from Bill. Sean Callahan lived here somewhere, but she didn't want another man yet. She'd work in a restaurant, but she wouldn't fall for the cook this time. She'd forget about the kids and everything they needed. If she talked to a kid now, it would be to say, *Do you want ketchup,* or *no, we don't give free refills.*

And then Mona said, "What do you think of Harlan?"

"He's all right." June opened the ashtray and looked inside. Sometimes you could find the end of a cigarette in there, but Mona was trying to quit and she shouldn't smoke in front of her anyway.

"Did you hear about the girl up here who got murdered for a snuff movie?" Mona asked.

June didn't want to talk about snuff movies. They had good news now, and for a minute she just wanted to think happy, relaxing thoughts. Was that so bad? Do you have to keep thinking of all the bad things every minute? Do you have to keep feeling sorry for so many people all the time?

She rolled the window down and pretended to concentrate on traffic.

In Catholic school, the nuns had told her that every time you say the phrase *Jesus, Mary, and Joseph, have mercy on their souls,* some poor suffering soul in Purgatory got to go to Heaven. She always imagined these poor, agonized souls waiting at a gate for someone to just say the words. It's such a small thing to ask. Just say the words, and they can be released from Purgatory, which is just like hell, only it is not eternal.

The school secretary's teenage daughter took medication for her obsessive thoughts, and June wondered what thoughts she had now instead, and if they seemed as real to her as her own thoughts, the ones she didn't have.

Mona was someone who said everything that came to mind. She read signs. She described the people in the cars around them, the houses they passed, the weather. Thoughts that a regular person would be embarrassed to find herself thinking were things Mona turned into conversation.

They pulled off the interstate and into town. They were only blocks away from the Hankses' house when Mona asked, "Do you think you'll get married again?"

"It's kind of early to think about that."

"I'd like to settle down again sometime, but I don't want any more kids. I already got two and that's enough." She paused and then added, "I thought their dad would remarry by now—he's a good catch, got himself the dairy farm job and all—but he hasn't. A boy needs a woman around, a mother type, you know. People say that about girls, but it's true for boys too."

They turned onto the Hankses' street. June searched eagerly for Cindy or Harlan, but no one was outside.

If she could talk to Cindy she could apologize. She'd tell Cindy that Bill was a good liar, and that he would have tricked her mother, just like he tricked her, and other women, and Cindy. She would try to explain what had happened, but she would not find excuses or say none of this was her fault. She would apologize to Cindy with all her heart because she meant it, and she wouldn't make excuses or blame anyone else. She would give Cindy the apology she had wished for herself. If she could just talk to her, then it would be better. Children always forgive, whether they should or not, they forgive and forgive.

She parked in front of the Hankses' house, and they got out of the car. The sound of their doors slamming brought Harlan outside, where he stood on the porch. He had a beer in his hand and he took a drink, watching them as they approached.

"Where the hell was she?" asked Mona. But he didn't answer. They knew where she had been. She was at the neighbor's house when he found her. She had once lived with her mother off Hawthorne Street, and that was where he had found her, playing with an old friend. "I hope you straightened her out," Mona said, but the relief showed on her face. "Damn kid."

June stayed on the sidewalk, but Mona walked up the stairs and onto the porch. She took a drink from Harlan's beer and gave it back again.

"She's sleeping now," Harlan told them.

The mention of sleep reminded the women of their own exhaustion, and now they yawned. Everyone needed to sleep. They had been up almost all night.

June started to offer Mona a ride home, but Mona didn't need a ride. She could stay here, if she wanted. She could go into Harlan's room and fold back his blankets and climb into his white sheets. She could do these things without thinking of them because they were just regular things as far as she was concerned, things she had done a hundred times before.

June said good-bye, but she didn't leave. They were finished with her, ready to go on, to go inside, to lie down and sleep together, to get up again later and carry on their lives without her. Mona went inside the house, but June didn't leave.

"I need to talk to Cindy," she called. She was on the sidewalk where she had stood the first day looking down at Harlan's legs as they stuck out from beneath a car. "I want to tell her how sorry I am."

Harlan walked to the edge of the porch and looked down at her. He didn't say anything for a minute, but just stood quietly. Then finally, he agreed. "She'd like that."

They stood, looking at each other. June wanted to come closer, but she didn't. "She's sleeping?"

Harlan moved toward the door. "Come on in."

She walked up the stairs and into the house. She passed Harlan's room. The door was open, but she didn't turn her head to look. She thought of the books by his bed—the history of Iraq, a mystery, and a manual on diesel motors. She didn't have a right to him, but somehow she felt that she did. It was wrong, but that was how she felt—that it should be her in his room right now, and not Mona.

June opened the door to Cindy's room and went inside. Cindy was sleeping, but when June sat beside her on the bed, she opened her eyes.

"I came to apologize," June said. She thought of the kids

at school who could never say they were sorry, but always wanted to excuse themselves and blame someone else. She thought of Bill: *you're not perfect either.* "I'm so sorry for lying to you."

Cindy narrowed her eyes. "You didn't even know her, did you?"

"No, I didn't know her."

"Were you mad because of Uncle Bill?"

"I didn't know about Bill and her."

Cindy considered this. "Mona said you were going to sell the story to a newspaper."

June shook her head. "I met Mr. Pruett the day he killed your mom. He offered me a ride, and when I wouldn't go with him, he got your mom instead."

"Instead of you." Cindy's eyes opened wide.

"I almost felt like it was my fault."

"It's Ralphie's father's fault. He's the one who did it. Mona says Ralphie will grow up to be just like him, but Uncle Harlan says he will not." Cindy still wore her clothes, a T-shirt and pants.

June didn't want to speculate about Ralphie Pruett's future, and she was quiet. There were things she had planned to say, but she couldn't think of them.

"It's because you don't have kids, Mona said."

"What do you mean?"

"It made you feel important to somebody."

"Mona said that?" It hadn't occurred to June, but now she thought Mona might have a point. She had stopped being important to Bill a long time ago.

"I know you stayed here with him," Cindy said quickly, not looking at her.

Harlan, she meant. June felt herself blush.

"I'm not shocked by it," Cindy assured her.

This was not the conversation June had imagined. "I don't usually lie to people," she said.

"Did Vernay know about you?"

June had promised herself she would be honest, but she lied. "No."

"Maybe she did, and she didn't care," insisted Cindy.

"Bill is a good liar." That, at least, was the truth.

Cindy was quiet. She rubbed her face and yawned.

"I won't be at school anymore," June said.

"In the kitchen?"

"I'm quitting."

"Are you leaving?"

"I think so."

"You know so?"

"Yeah."

"Are you just going to leave, or are you going to say good-bye first?"

June tucked the blankets around her. "First I'll say good-bye."

Chapter 29

S he drove home, and Bill was gone. She didn't look to see if dinner was in the refrigerator. It was warm outside, but she stayed in.

That night June called the school office and left a message on the phone saying she wouldn't be back. It wasn't right to leave her job like this, without warning, but it wouldn't be hard for them to replace her. They would find someone who didn't mind serving Cocoa Puffs and corn dogs, someone who knew how to put a boundary between herself and the kids, someone who would come to work and do her job. We always imagine no one can replace us, but we're wrong, she thought. We think no one can love the kids the way we do, but it's not true.

When it was time for bed, June undressed and turned out the light. It was a warm night, and she opened the window. She could smell the flowers outside, and the grass. She could hear cars in the distance. The streetlight had burnt out, and it was dark. When she turned her head, she could see stars. The thought crossed her mind that this was the last night in her bed, but she didn't dwell on it. She fell into a deep, black sleep.

The next day, June got up late and made herself coffee. She drank it sitting at the kitchen table. Bill's van was not there, but from where she sat, she could see his pile of things on the sidewalk.

She had forgotten how to understand what was happening. She had forgotten how to know what the truth was. She used to be a good judge of character. She was going to be careful now. She was going to pay attention. She was going to learn again how to tell the truth from a lie, to recognize pretense, to see what was genuine and move toward it. She wasn't going to fool herself anymore.

She would start over. You don't have to be Catholic for that. You can forgive yourself and begin again, fresh and pure, clean, white, perfect.

She had thought she would move to Portland, but now she wondered if there was another place she might choose, a place she hadn't thought of yet. If you could go anywhere— She and Cindy had played that game, but she couldn't remember what her own answer had been.

She didn't like it that people moved all the time. They left their homes. They left their parents and their little towns. They left everything they knew, like it didn't mean anything. Like they were too big for it. They left and went someplace new and started again. They left their husbands and their wives, and sometimes they left their children. What did they expect? she had always asked herself. Now she was one of them, and she still didn't have the answer.

June packed clothes and whatever food could be eaten without preparation. She didn't take much. She packed a few books. She could sell the car when she got where she was going. She could stay in a motel. She would get a job waiting tables. She was a good waitress. She had a good memory, and she was fast. She was patient and never yelled at the customers or acted like they were a pain in the ass. She could make good money. She was not like Vernay. She had manners and good grammar. She would not be too familiar with the customers or have an affair with the chef who was married. She thought she should be sad about leaving, but she wasn't.

She walked outside in the afternoon. It had rained hard earlier, but now the sun was out and the sky was blue. Her lupines were blooming and if she went around back, she would smell the honeysuckle. She hoped that whoever lived here next would take care of the flowers, but you could never tell about renters.

She drove to the bank and closed her account. She didn't have much money, and she'd need to be careful. She filled up her tank, and then she drove to the school. She pulled into the parking lot and parked. It was almost time for the bell.

She used to imagine taking one of the kids away with her. She used to think that about Mikey, that she'd take him away and they'd start a new life and she'd be the good mother, and he'd be her child. At least no zombies walk among us, he had told her.

She'd catch Cindy before she started walking home, and she'd give her a ride. Parents arrived to pick up their children. Hector's mother noticed June and waved. The bell rang. The doors flew open and the kids came out, running. They swarmed across the parking lot yelling and dropping their papers. They pushed, and some of them cried.

June got out of the car and searched the children's faces, but she didn't see Cindy. She saw Brittanee and Lural from Cindy's class and went to meet them. Where was Cindy? Had anyone seen her? Was she absent? But it was Thursday, they reminded her, and every Thursday Cindy and some of the other kids left school early to go to Thursday Club and learn about Jesus. It was held at the church down the street.

June started her car and pulled out of the lot. At Thursday Club, the kids got free Bibles. They got free clothes too, and coupons for McDonald's, and sometimes they went bowling, and once they got to see horses.

She drove past the church, but she was too late. Cindy would be inside.

She drove down the road, to the salvage yard where Harlan worked. She pulled into the lot next to a truck towing a smashed-up Geo Storm, and she hesitated. She adjusted the mirror and looked at herself. She put lipstick on and smoothed it with her finger, and then she opened the door and got out.

Inside, a line of six men stood working behind a long, dusty counter. Harlan was not one of them and for a sinking moment she thought she would never see either Harlan or Cindy again. She thought if she drove to their house it would be empty.

Each man at the counter stood in front of a computer on which he looked up parts: a distributor for a '92 Dodge, a transmission for an '86 Taurus station wagon. She heard the customers on each side of her making their requests. The place needed a good cleaning, but maybe the people who came here didn't care. She asked the man behind the counter if she could talk to Harlan Hanks, and he pointed to a door that led out back.

She walked through the door and outside, onto the back lot. From the front the salvage yard looked like a simple building with a tall fence around it, and that was all. But back here, it was another world, a world of smashed-up cars and trucks that stretched and wound as far as you could see. A landscape of calamities. She felt odd and out of place, but she began to walk. Men who worked here moved back and forth purposefully among the wreckage with no more concern on their faces than grocery store clerks.

She saw Harlan at last, squatting among those terrible cars, and she went to him. He was in the process of removing a tire from an old Mercury, and when he saw her he stood up. He had a rag stuck in his back pocket, and he pulled it out and wiped his hands. He waited for her to come close, and when she got there, he still waited.

"I'm leaving town today," she said, "and I'd like to talk to Cindy before I go." She looked down at her sandals, and they seemed wrong here. "I told her I'd say good-bye before I left." Maybe he'd say no. Maybe he thought it would be better if they could forget they ever saw her. Maybe her lies had erased everything else for him.

But when he finally spoke, he didn't say any of the things she feared. He said, "We got some news this morning."

She looked into his face.

"The cops came back again. And this time they said, they got that testing, DNA, you know, and what they found out, what they said, was that Pruett, he wasn't guilty. He's not the one."

"What?"

"They let him go."

"Let him go?"

"They found skin underneath her fingernails and it's not his."

June put her hand out on the car to steady herself. How could that be? Pruett with the blood in his car. Pruett stopping to help June, standing right next to her, thinking his awful thoughts. But then the woman had come out, and maybe she'd be able to identify him later. It's hard to identify people later, he must have known that. But still, it wasn't worth the chance. He had gone to her house to wait. But he didn't have to wait at all because there was Cindy's mother instead.

"If this is some little technicality—" June said.

But it wasn't a technicality. Ronald Pruett had not killed Vernay Hanks.

"Who could have done it?" Harlan asked, but June

wasn't ready to move away from Pruett's innocence. She leaned against the car. She braced her hands on the hot metal and spread her fingers out. They had the same color hair and the same build. They could have been sisters and wasn't that it, that he went for a certain look, their look? All the pieces had fit together, and now they had to come apart again. She looked at Harlan. Harlan had on a blue shirt, the color of his eyes. His name was written on the pocket, in cursive.

"There was the blood in his car," June reminded him.

And Harlan said, "He always admitted giving her a ride home."

He had given her a ride home. She had fought with Bill, but she had left Bill's house and gotten a ride with Pruett. At least, June thought, Bill wasn't the last one to see her. She had left their house and gotten a ride. At least that means it wasn't Bill. It was one thing to find out that your husband had sex with other women and quite another to discover that he killed them.

But Ralphie's father hadn't killed Vernay either. The police had made a mistake, and then she had read the article, and she had placed herself in the story when none of it had anything to do with her. She was irrelevant. The wife of the man the victim was visiting before she went off and got murdered, that's all. None of it was about her. Everything was built on a mistake. She had befriended the family. She had found out about Bill, and she had left him. She had lost everything.

"Why did it take so long?" she asked.

"What?"

"The DNA."

Harlan shrugged. "They made a mistake, lost something at first, I don't know. But it's not a technicality. Pruett is innocent and now I've got to tell Cindy that whoever killed her mom is still out there."

"So now it will go on and on," June said.

Harlan shrugged. "I don't expect it will go on too long." And then he added, "The police don't care much about a girl like Vernay."

But psychologically, she thought, it won't end. That's what she had read. If you don't know who did it, then you can't put it to rest.

"At least we know Bill didn't do it," he said, kindly.

"That's right," she said. "He would have never done something like that."

But Harlan said, "People are full of surprises."

They both looked at the ground. He wore black work boots, and they were dirty. He moved one of them over so that the tip touched her own naked toe.

Someone called for him. He was taking too long with that tire. He had to get back to work, he said, but he'd be home in an hour and so would Cindy. "Can you wait for us there?" He put his hand in his pocket, found the house key, and gave it to her. "I'll try to get away early."

She reached up to touch the writing on his shirt with her finger, tracing the letters. She had thought it was a hillbilly name at first, but what do we know about anything?

Chapter 30

She drove to the store and bought red wine, avocados, chicken, olive oil, tortillas, cheese, green peppers, onions, garlic, and enchilada sauce. She drove to the Hankses' house and parked out front. The neighbor's dog barked. She walked up the steps and onto the porch, and she let herself in. She went to the kitchen and set all the ingredients out on the counter. She found a pan under the sink and oiled it. She turned on the radio, to drown out the sound of the neighbor's dog. She heated the enchilada sauce. She sautéed the chicken and then she added the onions, the green pepper, and garlic. People think enchiladas are complicated, but they're not. She grated the cheese.

The man on the radio was talking about Judgment Day, and she changed the channel.

June set the table. She wished there were flowers to put in a vase, but there were no flowers here. She looked at the clock. If Harlan got off early, he could be home any minute.

She put the enchiladas in the oven to bake, and she

poured herself a glass of wine. She went out onto the front porch to have a cigarette. She sat on the stairs and waited. When they got home, they'd sit at the table and eat dinner. And afterward, they'd talk to Cindy together.

She thought of her Aunt Iva who got cancer and was supposed to die, but didn't. She thought of how Aunt Iva told her once that she never knew what it was to live until she thought she was going to die. June thought of Mikey Black and the other kids. She would miss them. She'd miss the kids and Bill. She'd miss sitting at the kitchen table, looking out. She'd miss the smell of honeysuckle. It's only when they're gone that we understand how truly sweet and precious these small things are, she thought.

Tomorrow she'd quit smoking. She'd get a restaurant job, she reminded herself. You can always fall back on waitressing. That's what everyone said. She smoked and sipped her wine. For Ralphie's sake, she should be glad that his father was innocent, but she wasn't. It messed up everything. She didn't know what to make of things now. Instead of being responsible for Vernay's death, Vernay had been responsible for the end of her own life, as she knew it. *Responsible* was the wrong word, but if there was a right word, she couldn't think of it.

It's irony, thought June. She had thought her life was miraculously saved that day, but instead that was the day everything had ended. If it wasn't for Cindy's mother, she'd be home now, sitting on her own back steps, eating dinner. She'd have a glass of wine. She'd be looking at her flowers, thinking, *I can't wait for Bill to come home.* They'd been married ten years, and that was still what she would have thought.

Across the street, the dog had twisted himself around the tree where he was tied, and he barked. Bark, bark, bark.

June put her cigarette out. She didn't understand how people could sit still while that dog barked. How could they stand it? If you call the police, they'll come by, but no one here called the police. She thought of Ralphie's father, and it was hard not thinking of him as the killer because she had imagined him like that for so long.

At the house across the street, the barks were now interspersed with yelps. The neighbor's old car sat in the driveway. Couldn't he hear his dog?

June stood up and walked down the steps. She hated to confront people, but sometimes it's our duty. A funny word, almost obsolete. She crossed the street. In Catholic school the nuns often talked about duty, but the idea had grown out of fashion. She would like to go someplace quiet. Maybe in a quiet place, a place without men, a place with no children or cars, she could begin to think clearly.

She crossed the street to the neighbor's yard. She passed the plastic Santa, lying on its side, and stopped in front of the dog. Should she unwind him from the tree herself? He was a rottweiler, originally trained to herd cows to market for the butchers in Germany. Mikey Black had written a paper about the breed, and he had told her what he had found out. All children are curious and get excited about the world and the facts and ideas of the world, even if their mothers put them in closets and burn their hands with cigarettes.

The dog barked at her, and she turned to go up the crooked steps. Rottweilers had almost become extinct at the turn of the century, when the butchers began to use trains to get cattle to market, but then someone had rescued the breed. She wondered where Mikey was now, this minute, and what he was doing and if anyone would think to rescue him. You weren't allowed to have contact with the children, in the place where they had taken him. She thought of Mikey walking through the woods with a dog, but that's not where he would be now. She thought, The things people need are not complicated.

The porch was full of garbage bags, and they smelled. It had old, wet newspapers on it, cigarette butts, empty aluminum cans and beer bottles. She knocked and waited. She would simply tell him that his dog needed his attention. Or she would say she heard his dog—how could she not? She would say, *I beg your pardon.* She would say, *I was just next door.*

She turned to look at the Hankses' house from here. She could see the front porch and the little yard. She could see the driveway, of course. She could see the window that had been Vernay's room, the room where Cindy now slept alone. The curtains were pulled back, and from here, if the lights were on, she'd be able to see inside. She knocked again. She wasn't going to think of Vernay, strangled with an electrical cord. The enchiladas would be ready in another ten minutes, and then, if possible, you let them sit for a while. They would taste even better tomorrow, but no one can wait a whole day for enchiladas.

She knew he was home.

She wouldn't have to say anything, really. She could just point to the poor dog. Surely anyone would be grateful to be told that his dog was strangling itself.

"You poor fellow," she said, and the dog wagged his tail. People said rottweilers could kill you in an instant. "You're a good dog, aren't you, buddy?" She thought of a boy who had once told her that he got his dog from Mexicans, and it only understood Mexican. Spanish, she had corrected him. *"Buenos dias, perro,"* she said.

The dog had begun to whimper, and she looked at him again, the thin cord twisted around the tree. She thought of what Mona had told her once, that the neighbor had yelled at his dog *if you don't shut up, I'll cut your head off.* What a thing to say. She rubbed her arms, and then her head swung to look again at the electrical cord around the dog's neck.

The door opened, and he was suddenly standing in front of her. He had not seen the expression on her face when she noticed the cord, and now she waited as if it was his turn to talk. She felt her ragged breath, and she told herself to slow it down. And with that thought, not just her breathing but everything slowed down so that time stretched out, frame by frame, like a cartoon drawing. She had all the time in the world as she stood on the porch looking at the man. He was small and muscular, with thick black hair on his arms. He had thin lips, a big nose, and blue eyes set too deeply into his face. He might not have been a bad-looking child. He would have had tiny pale hands. She thought of his hands now, close enough so that in an instant they could reach out and grab her. She didn't look at them, but she could feel their impatience, like little animals on a leash, pulling.

"Your dog," June said.

If he was an animal, he'd be a ferret.

She could smell liquor and sweat, and she could smell her own fear.

She motioned to the dog. "Your dog is twisted up, over there." And without looking away from the man, she added, "You better let him go, mister."

"I guess my dog is my own business."

He was a little man, a little weak bully of a man, the man who had caused all this. From here, he would have seen Vernay in her bedroom window. He would have seen Cindy and heard her childish games; seen Harlan in the driveway beneath a car, his legs sticking out. She wanted to say something big to the man, to put him in his place, to show him all that she thought and knew about him. He moved toward June with his hands out, but then suddenly behind her she heard singing and shouting. She heard the voices of children coming up the block, but she didn't turn away. It would be Cindy and her friends coming home from Thursday Club.

He had meant to pull her inside—she had seen it on his face—but it was too late. The kids had seen her. She could hear their voices, calling her name. She could hear Cindy, loudest of all.

June's eyes hadn't left his face. "If you won't take care of that dog," she said, "you ought to give him to someone who will."

"That dog could bite your head off."

June could hear the children coming up behind her. He couldn't do anything now. A moment ago he had her but now, because of the children, he was defenseless. She looked at the dog. It was a young dog and, seeing her look, it lowered its head and front legs and then jumped up, barking.

"That cord you got on his neck—it's too tight," she said. She had been through too much to be afraid of him.

Cindy had come up beside June on the porch. She had heard this last remark, and she said, "I seen a TV show about people who let their dogs' collars get too tight and the skin grows right over. Somebody has to cut it out with a knife, a vet has to do it. You can get in trouble for that. They'll send someone out and give you a ticket."

"It's not a collar," said the man.

"No, it's not," agreed June. "It's an electrical cord." She met his eyes, and then, putting her hand around Cindy's arm, turned to walk back across the street.

They were on the sidewalk in front of Harlan's house when June stopped and looked back. He was standing where she had left him, still watching her. "Cindy, go in and get the phone," she said. She suddenly remembered the enchiladas. "Turn off the oven while you're in there, would you?"

June sat down on the front steps. She found a cigarette in her pocket and lit it. She slid her shoes off. The man across the street went back inside his house, slamming the door behind him.

Cindy returned with the telephone. "You made enchiladas! You said you would and you did." She sat next to June with Little Babe on her lap. "Now you have to stay for supper."

June had planned to call the police, but what could she tell them? Besides the electrical cord, what was there to go on? Her intuition? The feeling she got when she stood at his door and turned to look at Vernay's bedroom window? The way he looked at her or his tone of voice?

"Cindy, there are more good people in the world than there are bad ones," June said. "Always remember that." His hands had started to move toward her, but then the kids had interrupted.

"Are you going to call about the dog?" Cindy slipped her fingers beneath Little Babe's collar, feeling the space there. "If they took the dog away from him, would they give it to someone else, or would they put it to sleep?"

When June didn't answer, Cindy added, "I could take him."

Harlan would be home any minute. She could feel the man watching from his house, but she wasn't afraid.

"I'd take him," Cindy repeated.

"That dog's probably mean," said June absently.

"Because the man's so mean to it? He's mean and so they kill it—that's not fair. That's not fair!"

June turned to look at her, a little girl holding a fat Chihuahua on her lap. "We'll see about the dog. Okay?"

"On the TV someone called about a dog that had its collar grow into its skin, and they came out and got it. A vet had to cut that collar off, poor dog. You can call if somebody is mean to a dog and they'll come out, I'm telling you." The phone was on the step next to Cindy.

"I've got to think things through," said June. "I've got to talk to your uncle—"

When Cindy started to interrupt, June held up her hand and the girl was quiet.

From his house across the street, the neighbor would have seen Vernay coming and going, heard the music she played, smelled her cooking. On warm nights she might have sat outside on the steps. He would have known all these things about her and it wasn't enough, still it wasn't, to make her mean anything. She didn't mean anything to him, none of them did. He was a little bully and it didn't seem right, it flew in the face of all that was fair and right, that he could have been the instrument of so much.

"Look! Here comes my uncle," called Cindy.

June smashed out her cigarette, slipped her shoes on, and stood up. She watched as Harlan drove toward them, parked his car at the curb, opened the door, and stepped out. It was late afternoon, but the day had kept its warmth.

She could feel the man across the street at his window. She could hear children's voices down the street and a radio from someone's house. June hesitated, but then Harlan called her name, and she moved forward to meet him.

Acknowledgments

I'd like to thank those who made this book possible. Thank you to my sister, Tamara Taylor, for your advice. Thanks to my children, Charlotte Willer and Sasha Clement, each a source of endless ideas, and to my tireless readers: Madeleine Madar and Barbara Loeb. Thanks to my agent, Candice Fuhrman, for your hard work and friendship. I'd also like to thank Wendy Walker, my enthusiastic editor. Thank you Sara Backer, for all you've taught me about writing. Thank you also to the Corvallis peace community and to the children of the school where I work. Thanks to Kris Kleindienst, Bob Rossi, Matthew Roudané, Rachel Cole, Thom Chambliss, Pat Starker, and Susan Klinkhammer. Thank you Penelope Kaczmarek. And, of course, thank you to my partner, Chuck Willer, for everything you do.